Lady Charlotte's Ruined Marquess

THE HEIR AND THE SPARE
BOOK TWO

FIONA MIERS

Copyright © 2024 by Fiona Miers

All rights reserved.

No part of this book may be reproduced in any form or by any electronic or mechanical means, including information storage and retrieval systems, without written permission from the author, except for the use of brief quotations in a book review.

Prologue

Ten years earlier

"Your father wishes to see you, Archibald," the Marchioness of Hunting announced to the quiet room in which they sat, her red-rimmed eyes puffy and fragile looking.

Archie's once-happy heart dropped so low, he was surprised he couldn't see it lying on the carpet at his feet.

He dragged himself out of his chair and walked the few steps across the room to the heavy wooden door that marked the entrance to his father's domain.

His trepidation was almost crippling. His hands shook, and his desire to run away was so strong that Archie had to lock his knees in place so that he didn't obey what his instincts were screaming at him to do. He hung his head for a moment, squeezed his eyes shut, then released a long breath.

It was time to face his destiny.

He lifted his head and stared at the mahogany wood, raising his still shaking hand and knocking on his father's study door.

"Enter." His father's hoarse voice sounded through the solid barrier and Archie squared his shoulders.

Archie turned the silver knob, pushed open the door and saw another set of red-rimmed eyes, matching his mother's.

Archie gasped and bowed low to his father to disguise his surprise. His father couldn't have been crying, surely? There had to be another reason for his appearance. Perhaps it was the result of heavy drinking and fatigue? Archie could only hope.

"Sit down, Archibald," his father commanded, his strong voice croaking and rough.

Archie almost tripped over the rug in his haste. His father had never before asked him to be seated in his presence. He had certainly never used his Christian name before in such a way. Archie could only hope that his father might be about to comment on his upcoming birthday, although his detached and logical brain knew that this thought didn't fit in with the visible tears which he had seen his cold, aloof mother and his proud, drunken father shed.

"Archibald, we have received some bad news and it seems that your brother will no longer be inheriting the Marquisate."

This life-altering statement was delivered with all the excitement of a eulogy. Archie's father had always been proud of his eldest son. It had been obvious in both his actions and words. Archie's older brother was the charismatic, arrogant and handsome heir who had always looked and acted just like their father.

He cleared his throat and tugged on his cuff. "Pardon, sir? Do you mean that Arthur will not be inheriting?"

"Do not speak back to me!"

Shock ricocheted through his system, yet he schooled his features into an expression of proper regard with practiced ease. He had spent the last five years as part of a group of four youths referred to as 'The Spares.' The four members were all the second sons of rich, old and powerful families. None of these friends wanted their father's title, nor the responsibility that came with it. Archie felt the same way. To be told that he would have to forget all his plans for the future, of managing his money and breeding horses, was devastating. He felt sick to his stomach.

"My apologies, sir." Archie bobbed his head in a seated half-bow, his head spinning with questions. What was he going to do now?

He sat still and waited for his father to continue. He needed more information, but with the unbalanced mood his father was in, Archie knew better than to push.

The older man appeared to be mulling the words over in his head, twirling his empty liquor glass around in his hands.

"Arthur is dying. He has indulged in his taste for loose women far too freely and now he is going to die."

His father shook his head sadly.

Archie was completely shocked. If he had been standing, he doubted he would still have been upright. Was his brother dying? He knew Arthur had not been feeling well recently, but dying? And from the dreaded French disease? Archie was not close to his older brother, as there was more than six years between them, but he didn't want him to die.

Whilst Archie was trying to digest this new information, his father hit him with the next verbal sledgehammer.

"So, you keep yourself clean. Understand me? Stay away from the whores and make sure you marry a woman who will be able to handle the scandal when it comes. We will be sending your brother to Italy for an extended holiday, but if word ever gets out, the family's reputation will be ruined."

Archie felt his heart stop. Was his father asking him to stay away from women? For how long? His friends had already organised his eighteenth birthday. A night of drinking and his first time in a brothel, his first female.

Did his father mean that he couldn't bed a woman until he married?

As Archie's mind raced with the implications of what his father had told him, he felt his heart slowly disappear. It shriveled up, just like a grape left on the vine too long.

His father was telling him that he was to inherit everything. The estate, the servants, the title, the responsibility. Everything, including a name that would forever be remembered for his brother's grotesque death. The society in which Archie wanted to be accepted would soon scorn him. What woman would want him? As Archie thought about all the lost possibilities, he realised that his life would never be the same again.

Chapter One

London 1812

Lord Archibald Turner, Archie to his friends, was the second son of the Marquess of Hunting. Archie had spent the last decade living an exemplary life. The epitome of gentlemanly behaviour, habits, and dress, without any of the excesses frowned upon but secretly tolerated.

He hardly drank, he didn't gamble, and he was a twenty-seven-year-old virgin. This, of course, meant he had never compromised anyone and had never taken advantage of the offers which were passed his way by the many unhappily married women of the *ton*. Archie spent more money on his clothes than all his friends combined, but that meant he always looked attractive and civilized.

Archie had spent the last six years fighting an intense attraction for one amazing woman. She was the only person who noticed him as more than the holy saint he pretended to be. She fought with him in public, teased him blatantly and laughed her full-bodied laugh at him. She was the only woman he had ever loved, and he wasn't sure how much longer he could bear standing close to her without declaring his intentions.

Lady Charlotte Dunford.

Archie groaned as his wayward member stiffened in response to said woman's laugh and the accompanying wobble of her generous breasts. He was wearing dark grey breeches that were so tight, they revealed everything. Archie had muscular thighs, unlike most of the men of the *ton* and his tailor often had trouble cutting his breeches just right. This wasn't usually a problem, but when the front of his breeches was quite visible due to a high-waisted, white waistcoat and cut away evening jacket, Archie began to panic. Desperate for something that would douse his ardour, he thought back to the last time he had seen Charlotte.

It had been almost nine months before.

Archie had been standing with his friend of over fifteen years, the former Lord Oliver Lyre, now the Duke of Lincoln. Oliver had shown up to a *ton* ball, without his new wife. Oliver had been explaining why his wife was in Scotland, rather than by his side in London, when Charlotte had become incensed and started scolding him in the middle of a crowded ballroom.

Lady Charlotte Dunford, his heart, his soul, the only woman Archie would ever want to marry. She was the only daughter of the Duke of Arrow, his friend, Lord John Dunford's younger sister, and the most beautiful woman Archie had ever seen. She was also a woman with a keen mind and a nasty temper when aroused, and unfortunately, Oliver had excited it that night.

"You've done what?" Lady Charlotte raised her voice at the Duke, casting angry eyes heavenward and then fixing them back on Oliver's face.

Archie wanted to put his hands over his ears to block the sound but gallantly squashed that ungentlemanly urge.

"Lady Charlotte, please," Oliver said.

Archie wasn't sure why Oliver, Duke of Lincoln, had let his duchess, Sarah, leave him to go to Scotland, but he felt perfectly sure that a public reprimand was not the way to go about finding out.

It was a pity that Lady Charlotte hadn't felt the same way.

"You've done what?" Lady Charlotte spat at him, quieter this time.

She removed the scowl from her face and plastered on her polite facade. Society did not approve of displays of excessive emotion and frowned upon public spectacles. Archie watched Lady Charlotte's attempt to conceal her feelings and could have told her not to bother. Lady Charlotte, having been a spoilt and indulged only daughter, had never been forced to school her features. She was, therefore, atrocious at pretending to feel calm when she felt otherwise.

"I returned to London without my wife." The duke repeated the words, obviously upset to be admitting the fact. His face flushed, his gaze darting around the room.

"And you packed her off to a Scottish castle? Your new wife? Your duchess?" Lady Charlotte enunciated each word calmly. Her expression was remote, but her words dripped venom. Archie held his breath. This was going to get very ugly, very quickly.

"She wanted to go. She wasn't enjoying living on the estate, and when I asked her whether she wanted to come back to London with me, or stay there, she chose to travel to Scotland instead."

Archie found this rather odd. He knew Oliver's wife, Sarah, and had seen the couple on their wedding day. Unlike most couples of the *ton*, who married for financial or social reasons, Oliver and Sarah's marriage had been a love match. Why had it gone wrong so quickly?

"What did you do?" Lady Charlotte asked again.

Archie could see the anger in Charlotte's eyes, he could feel the current of rage in her body, as though it was his own. He had always been able to do that. He could read her like no one else seemed able to do, not even her brother.

"I didn't do a thing. The servants welcomed her, and I took the utmost care to ensure her comfort. When my mother and sister-in-law arrived, they tried to—"

"No!" Lady Charlotte exploded.

Archie heard Oliver's groan and wished he could do the same thing. Must she always be so passionate about everything?

"You let your mother and that *snake* of a sister-in-law visit you while you were on your honeymoon?" Charlotte was incredulous.

"They didn't visit. They live there."

Charlotte seemed shocked by Oliver's reasoning, and Archie knew she didn't understand. She would never know what it was like to feel like you weren't wanted or needed by your parents. Once upon a time, he had felt the same way and it seemed that Oliver still did. Why else would he have allowed his relatives to invade what should have been his home?

"Oh, Sarah, you poor, poor thing." Lady Charlotte murmured to herself, clasping her hands to her breasts.

"Lady Charlotte, that is not fair. I didn't do anything." Oliver protested again. Archie could have told him it was pointless.

"Exactly. You didn't do anything to protect your beautiful, sweet, innocent wife from being set upon by the most cunning, jealous pair of women I have ever met."

Archie raised an eyebrow, wondering which woman other than the dowager duchess that Lady Charlotte meant. Probably Lady Honoria, Oliver's sister-in-law.

"You stupid, ignorant–" As Lady Charlotte started to wind herself up into a full-blown attack, Archie gathered his courage and quickly stepped into the line of fire.

"Lady Charlotte," he interrupted, moving in front of Oliver and bowing to her. "May I have the honour of this dance?"

Lady Charlotte shut her mouth and eyed Archie with disdain. Archie made sure his body language left her no room for argument, and he stood in a way that completely blocked Oliver from her line of vision.

"Of course, my lord," she managed, her eyes flashing daggers around him at Oliver even while Archie led her away.

Her hand on his arm felt like a burning flame to his coat. He had avoided dancing with her since her coming out ball and this was the reason why. He had always hoped that his reaction to her would diminish; hoped his body would learn not to be so sensitive to her, but it had never happened.

She had as much effect on him today, as every other day since he'd met her.

Archie pulled Lady Charlotte gently into a waltz position–it had to be a waltz, bloody bad luck—and started moving her expertly around the room. Neither of them had spoken yet, but her eyes spoke volumes. Lady Charlotte had now divided her anger and Archie wasn't sure if he would fare worse or better than Oliver.

"Go on. I know you want to," Archie encouraged, schooling his face into his usual mask of politeness. He had thought that after a decade of pulling this face, it would be second nature and no longer feel false. But when he was with Charlotte, every feeling was intensified, to the point of being almost painful.

"I have nothing to say."

Archie bit back a smile. Lady Charlotte never addressed him, never had. He found it quite funny. He had no title, so she couldn't refer to him like that. He had never given her leave to call him Archie, and yet having been around her brother for most of her life, she could call him anything she wanted. And yet Lady Charlotte didn't. She avoided referring to him at all, and if she was pressed, she occasionally called him 'my lord,' with a wry twist to her lips.

Charlotte's expressions were transparent. Archie could see every thought, every feeling as they crossed her face. At the moment, though, it didn't take a person familiar with Lady Charlotte to deduce her feelings. Her rage was there for the whole world to see. Her face flushed, her eyes narrowed and sparked with passion.

"Lady Charlotte," Archie began. She hissed at him through her clenched teeth.

He had always addressed her as Lady Charlotte, partly because it was her title, due her because of her fortunate birth, but also partly because it annoyed her. For the first time since Archie had met Charlotte, he didn't ignore her glare.

"Well, what would you like me to call you?" he snapped, letting some of his annoyance slip into his voice. Lady Charlotte's lips parted and her eyes widened, measurably. Archie didn't know if it was due to the tone of his voice or from his wording, but he couldn't take the words back now.

She opened her mouth to reply, then shut it again.

Archie waited. He danced them around the room, and he waited some more. Charlotte looked beautiful when she was angry. Her too-full lips parted slightly, and her bluer-than-blue eyes gave him a penetrating look, as if she was trying to read him. He knew she wouldn't see anything revealing on his face, but it never seemed to stop her from trying to understand him.

"Charlotte," she answered finally, her eyes wary as she awaited his response.

"Well, Charlotte, say what you are thinking, so you can feel better."

Archie tightened his hold on her reflexively, as he feared she would leave him on the dance floor if she got angry with him.

"May I call you Archie?" She burst out with this question, instead of answering him.

He almost laughed out loud and smiled, despite himself. He had meant that she should vent her anger at him, not ask for his permission to use his name.

"Of course." He inclined his head. Her spine stiffened again, her hand going rigid in his grasp.

He groaned internally. Why was it that everything he did seemed to annoy her?

"Archie, how dare you pull me away just because I was angry with Oliver? He deserves to know what an imbecile he is. Doesn't he realise that Sarah will be heartbroken that he has abandoned her for his pursuits in London?"

Archie frowned. How could Charlotte know this?

"Firstly, I did not pull you away. I asked you to dance." He tightened his hold on her hand, as though to illustrate the point.

"For the first time in five years," Charlotte muttered under her breath, looking down and away from him. "And right at that moment."

Archie inhaled against the sudden pain in his chest. She sounded upset that he hadn't danced with her regularly over the years. If only she'd known the torment he felt every time another man held her, she wouldn't have been so quick to chastise him about the time they had spent apart.

Chapter Two

Ignoring her jibe, Archie continued. "Secondly, how can you be so sure of Sarah's feelings?"

Was this something ladies discussed? Or was Charlotte making assumptions?

"Because that was always Sarah's biggest fear about marrying above her station. The day before they married, she told me that she would never survive if Oliver chose another woman over her, if he took a mistress, or decided to gallivant around London instead of being with her. He is not only doing that, but he made sure she was in a different country, where she can only assume the worst."

In typical Charlotte fashion, she was not only discussing a topic that any unmarried lady of breeding would avoid, but she also spoke with such passion that Archie wished he could kiss her, suck on her lips until they bruised.

Archie closed his eyes as the longing coursing through him made him want to drop to his knees and beg her to be his. He slowed their dancing as the orchestra stopped, his palms beginning to sweat. One day, he would do something very foolish when it came to Charlotte. He could only hope it didn't occur in a ballroom full of people.

"Charlotte, if you'd like, I could speak to Oliver. I don't believe he is happy to be away from his wife."

Archie led Charlotte away from the dance floor, dropping her hand as quickly as he could.

"It doesn't matter whether he's happy or not. She must be miserable."

And with that declaration, she stormed off.

Archie suddenly came back to the present with a jolt and smiled to himself at the memory he'd just been reliving. He recalled that had been the last time he had enjoyed a real conversation with Charlotte.

It was now nine months later; the beginning of another season, and she was miraculously still unattached. Archie watched her twirl around the room in the arms of a wealthy young lord and found himself wishing she would get married so he could also find someone suitable to marry. He could never commit himself to another until she was settled. It didn't make sense of course, but Archie couldn't bring himself to marry while Charlotte, the one and only woman he had ever really desired, was still available.

"Archie." Oliver approached with a genuine smile and shook his hand with vigour. Oliver was wearing a rose-coloured waistcoat, a black evening coat, and breeches. The ensemble sat very well on him.

Archie smiled warmly, his heart lifting at the sight of the Duke of Lincoln. His friend had never looked better, or happier.

"You look well, Oliver. How are things?" Archie asked the question more out of politeness than for any other reason, as he already knew that everything was well.

"Excellent. Thanks to your advice, my finances have never been better, and my new estate manager has everything running smoothly."

Oliver had been the second son of the late Duke of Lincoln, and he had once confided to Archie that his father had told him he would never inherit, so there was no reason to teach him anything about being a duke.

So, when at twenty-five years of age, Oliver had unexpectedly inherited the estate, he'd had no idea how to manage anything, let alone a dukedom. He had floundered considerably. Not only concerning the needs of his property and his many dependents including servants and tenants, but also concerning his position in society, where he was expected to fulfill the role of a duke to the manor born.

"And your family?" Archie asked, grinning widely at his friend.

"Sarah's extremely well, thank you, and my son is wonderful."

The pleasure that Oliver felt in those words was apparent. Sarah, his beautiful wife, glided up at that moment, her rose silk gown complementing her husband's attire. She slid her hand into the crook of her husband's elbow and Oliver seemed to glow like the stars.

"Archie," Sarah greeted him warmly, her smile mirroring her husband's.

"Your Grace." Archie couldn't resist addressing the lady before him with her new title, bowing deeply over Sarah's outstretched hand and placing a chaste kiss on her knuckles.

Sarah blushed crimson, the colour extremely becoming on her. She had been born a clergyman's daughter, and Archie knew that she was still a little overwhelmed about the title she had gained upon her marriage to Oliver.

She tapped at him playfully with her fan, reminding him that he should address her only by her first name. Archie laughed. His friend was very lucky.

Across the room, Lady Charlotte Dunford watched the scene between Archie and their mutual friends, the Duke and Duchess of Lincoln, with a warmth heating her face. She averted her eyes.

Why did Archie never tease her like that? Why did he never smile at her like he was smiling at the duchess right now? Because he thinks you're a spoilt little girl, the cynical voice in her head reminded her.

Archie had been friends with her brother, Lord John Dunford, since Charlotte had been a child. Five years younger than John, she had been barely eight years old when she first met Archie. She had thought him polite, but nothing more. At eight years of age, she wasn't interested in boys and her brother's solemn friend had not commanded her attention. When she had reached sixteen and became a debutante, she had seen Archie as the man he was. Twenty-one years old, handsome as sin and as proud as a peacock.

He had danced with her once. As her brother's friend, he had been obliged to ease her way into society by offering to dance with her. Charlotte had felt safe with him, knowing he wasn't assessing her suitability as the perfect wife, as some of the more mature gentlemen had been. He had been polite but distant, and he had kept that distance for six years.

No, that was untrue. This dawned on Charlotte as she reflected on their association. They had also danced once, the previous year. Charlotte sighed at the memory.

She recalled how she had been furious at Oliver. Archie had whisked her away to prevent her from scolding his friend in public and thereby creating a spectacle. Archie was loyal to those he loved; he always had been. John always said that you could count on Archie to do the right thing, no matter the cost to himself.

During that waltz, Charlotte had finally seen a little of the real emotion Archie could express, which she had been looking for since she'd been a young girl. He had cracked open his mask for just a moment, and she had been shocked almost speechless. Lord Archibald Turner was not a heartless machine, it seemed. He had feelings; she just wasn't sure how many, or exactly what they meant. Either way, he had captured her attention that night.

Now, raising her social armour and breezing across the ballroom, she approached the young Duchess of Lincoln with her traitorous heart beating at a fast pace in her ears.

"Charlotte!" Sarah cried happily, her whole face lighting up.

She looks so well, was Charlotte's first thought. Sarah had always been slightly pale and a little thin, but now she glowed with happiness and was nicely plump after giving birth to her son just three months previously. She was also wearing a rose silk gown that beautifully complemented her creamy skin and blonde hair, not to mention the newly acquired curve of her bosom, which only added to her beauty.

Charlotte leaned forward and gave the Duchess of Lincoln a quick hug.

"Sarah, I have missed you," she told her friend honestly. She hadn't seen Sarah in almost a year, not since her wedding. Sarah had disappeared on her honeymoon and then hadn't returned to London. Until now.

Sarah's eyes glistened slightly and then she smiled brightly.

"I have missed you too, although I do remember a particular invitation from Scotland that you declined." She teased her friend, poking her lightly with her fan.

Charlotte suppressed a sigh. She would have loved to visit Scotland after Sarah's baby had been born, but the combination of envy for her happiness and respect for the young couple's need for privacy had kept Charlotte in London.

"I would have loved to visit you, my friend, but I know how much you enjoy having your husband to yourself," she replied, giving Oliver a sharp glance.

The duke looked at the floor in obvious embarrassment. He must have recalled that the last time he had seen Charlotte, she had railed at him for leaving Sarah in Scotland.

She smiled to herself. Good. He should feel bad about that. It had been a dreadful thing to do to his new wife.

"We all know that you never leave London, however odd that is, Lady Charlotte. Scotland would be far too uncivilized for you." Archie's cold voice broke into the conversation and Charlotte's gaze turned to him. Was he trying to make her look selfish in front of Sarah?

"Lord Archibald, good evening, sir," she replied haughtily, giving Archie a half-curtsey.

He bowed low in return. He was a marquess' son, but he was the second son, and she was the daughter of a duke. As they were both unmarried, she outranked him.

"I rarely leave London, it is true, but I would have loved to visit Sarah," she repeated, daring him to contradict her again.

Archie would usually have ignored any attempt to bait him, yet tonight, she seemed to succeed while barely trying.

"How can you say that you would have loved to have ventured to Scotland when you rarely even visit Hampshire in the off season?" he challenged, with a raised eyebrow.

"That's only because..." Charlotte began to explain, until her brother, Lord John Dunford cleared his throat, stopping her in mid-sentence.

She sighed loudly. John was correct. She could hardly divulge that by tacit understanding between her parents, her father took his long-time mistress to the country estate every year once the Season was over, while Charlotte and her mother stayed in London. It was common enough knowledge that her father had a mistress, but no one knew just how much time the duke spent with her.

How could she tell Archie why she couldn't leave London if John didn't want him to know?

"You are right, Lord Archibald, how remiss of me to forget how shallow I am."

Sarah gasped, but Charlotte ignored her, focusing instead on Archie. Although most of the time she hated him, part of her loved their exchanges. No one saw her as more than a wealthy duke's daughter, to be caught for marriage and used for her hostess skills, and to provide an heir. Those wanting to marry her included false flattery and flummery when they spoke to her. Archie never did any of that. Even if he only noticed her flaws, she liked how he treated her as a person, not as the daughter of a wealthy duke.

"Not shallow, Lady Charlotte, only too self-centred and focused on London," Archie replied, injecting humour into his voice.

Charlotte ignored the humour. She didn't want to smile and laugh with him. For some reason, she got a perverse pleasure out of sparring with Archie in public, and she wouldn't be backing down.

"Oh, *self-centred*? Really? Even better." She snorted inelegantly.

Archie just smiled at her, in a most agreeable manner. That annoyed her even more than a cutting reply would have done.

Charlotte had just opened her mouth for a blistering rejoinder when Sarah intervened.

"How is your brother, Archie?" Sarah asked, linking her arm with Charlotte's.

Charlotte looked down at Sarah's hand and realised she was being cautioned to be quiet. She noticed Archie's face pale slightly and wondered why.

"He is not so well. I thank you for asking, Duchess," he murmured. Sarah leaned forward and tapped him with her fan again.

He smiled reluctantly and fixed his mistake. "Sarah," he said.

Charlotte inhaled sharply at the exchange. How did Sarah know how to tease him, to make him smile? And to accept his teasing in return?

All Charlotte knew how to do was to annoy him—or get annoyed at him. Maybe she should try hitting him with her fan? Her fingers tightened reflexively on her new silk adornment, holding back the impulse. She knew she could never flirt so blatantly with Archie.

"What ails your brother?" Charlotte asked, wondering what everyone else knew that she didn't.

Archie's posture went rigid as he met her gaze. He had the most beautiful brown eyes.

"Arthur left for a grand European trip almost ten years ago. After a few years of travel, he came down with a lung illness which has kept him overseas. The doctors believe that the damp British climate will only worsen his condition."

Archie spoke so stiffly that it seemed a rehearsed speech.

How many times had he repeated that exact phrase? Was his brother so unwell? Still?

"So, is that where you disappear to every year once the season is over?" Charlotte didn't think about how much that question would reveal about her.

Archie gave her a quizzical look, but instead of answering, just inclined his head.

Charlotte flushed and tried her best to conceal her discomfort.

"I must go. Mother said she wanted to leave early tonight." Charlotte excused herself and moved away from the group, promising Sarah she would visit soon.

When she looked back, only one person was looking at her. Archie.

Chapter Three

The next day was a Saturday, and Charlotte needed to speak to her father about her birthday ball. Money was not among the acceptable subjects of discussion in her family, but she had decided to hire a second French chef to help with the catering and thought perhaps she should consult her father first.

Finding no sign of him in his usual place, the library, Charlotte located her mother in her sitting room, writing a letter.

"Is Father not at home, Mother?"

Her mother's shoulders stiffened and she knew what the answer was going to be. *Oh, dear!* Why hadn't she just asked the butler?

"He's gone to his whore." Her mother turned in her chair and beckoned Charlotte inside the room with a flick of her bony finger.

Her father had long ago established a mistress in a different part of town. As long as she could remember, she had been discreetly aware of the woman's existence. It had always seemed odd to her that her father had kept the same woman for so long. Charlotte thought that the idea of a gentleman having a mistress would be to change them regularly, for variety. But what did she know?

"Oh, I'm sorry, Mother." It was her automatic response and she steeled herself for the emotional onslaught that would surely follow.

"Why are you sorry, Charlotte? It is not your fault that your father is an ordinary man. No man ever stays faithful to his wife. You have been clever to remain unmarried for so long."

Charlotte's eyebrows rose. Inwardly, her belly squirmed in an uncomfortable way. Her mother thought that her not marrying was a good thing? Although she had never been pushed into marrying any of the men who had proposed to her, she had always felt that she was letting her mother down in some way. Obviously, she had been wrong.

"Oliver is faithful to Sarah," Charlotte murmured, dipping her head to avoid her mother's eyes.

Her mother made a very unladylike noise, close to a snort.

"That is only because she is little better than a whore herself."

Charlotte gasped. How could her mother say such a thing?

"Mother! Sarah is a beautiful person." It was true that most men of Oliver's standing would have made Sarah their mistress rather than marry her, but Sarah had been brought up as a lady.

"She is little better than a servant, Charlotte. I can only imagine that he married her because she tricked him into it. He may be faithful now, as they've only been married for a year, but give it time."

Her mother was smiling rather wickedly now, her lips turned up in a wider smile than Charlotte had seen in years.

Charlotte couldn't imagine Oliver ever wanting another woman whilst he had Sarah. But then again, didn't her mother have more experience in these things? What man stayed faithful his whole married life? Which gentleman didn't have one mistress, or even more than one? She knew John did, and it was even whispered that her older brother, Cyril, had a wife and a mistress. Maybe her mother was right, and it was just a matter of time for Oliver and Sarah. The thought brought sadness to Charlotte's heart.

"You have done very well, Charlotte. A woman can enjoy being her own mistress. You need never know the humiliation of the marriage bed nor the pain of childbirth."

Charlotte stifled her sigh.

"So, you are happy for me never to marry, then, Mama?" Charlotte asked cautiously.

She couldn't believe she was having this conversation. Every mother she knew was practically throwing their daughters down the aisle, yet her mother didn't care one way or the other? Or even more extreme—preferred her daughter *not* to wed?

"Of course, I would like to see you marry, Charlotte. It is a woman's greatest achievement. But there are very few eligible, titled gentlemen available, and I refuse to allow you to marry below your rank."

Charlotte paled. If that was the case, then she'd probably never marry. There were few, if any, unmarried dukes in London nowadays.

Her mother continued. "You will never want for anything, as I'm sure your brother will continue to support you throughout your life. As your father does now."

Charlotte nodded, feeling her cheeks grow hot.

So, it was true, then. Her mother, apparently like all women before her, had only married so she could improve her station in life.

Charlotte had always believed she would marry for love, and had hoped to find a man with whom she could have a good, amicable relationship on which to build a steady love. A marriage based on mutual affection and not just the joining of two wealthy families.

Men like Oliver could marry almost anyone. They could choose a woman for her beauty, her bloodlines, or her dowry. Most women married the man who could make their lives comfortable.

But Charlotte had been born into a noble family, and few women of the *ton* had the comfort and resources she enjoyed. She had already been bestowed with some personal wealth by her father, and even had a small country estate of her own, which was currently leased.

As the daughter of a duke, she had high status in society. By the *ton*'s standards, she would gain nothing of worth from marrying. However, the man who managed to win her hand in marriage would gain significantly.

An inner part of her knew that nothing short of unconditional love would tempt her into marriage. But unlike the case of Sarah, the young

Duchess of Lincoln, most men would look at Lady Charlotte Dunford and see only what they could acquire.

Curtseying to her mother, she left the room with a new sense of inevitability and a heavy sinking feeling in the pit of her stomach.

~

A WEEK LATER, it was the day of Charlotte's ball.

After Archie had pointedly sent her flowers on her real birthday, rather than on the actual day of her ball as everyone else had the year before, Charlotte had chosen to celebrate on her actual birthday. Archie would have nothing to complain about this time.

She had been secretly thrilled when his bouquet of flowers had arrived this morning. All her other friends and admirers chose expensive, well-known and therefore common flowers. Archie, as always, had chosen something memorable. A bouquet of yellow daffodils and a posy of pale pink rosebuds.

Charlotte wanted to take them up to her room and leave all of the everyday white and red roses in the foyer. Instinct told her that this would be too much cause for gossip. In the end, she told the footmen to take several bouquets to her room, including the daffodils.

As the day wore on, she found herself daydreaming about dancing with Archie at the ball that night. A fantasy indeed, as it would be a miracle for Archie to do such a thing.

That evening, she stood at the entrance to the ballroom to welcome her guests. Her parents stood beside her until most of the guests had arrived, and then excused themselves to retire to their respective domains. Her mother, to her group of friends, and her father disappeared in the opposite direction.

The room was comfortably full, and now that she had fulfilled some of her hostess duties, she walked through the ballroom speaking to people and accepting their congratulations. She was talking to Sarah, Oliver, their friend Rupert and her brother John when her skin prickled, and she turned to see *him*.

Archie had been making his way to Oliver's side without noticing her. The shock that registered on his face when he realised she was within speaking distance was almost comical. He bowed politely, wished her a happy birthday and then stood as far away from her as he could, while still within their circle.

"What about you, little sister? You're getting closer to being labelled as 'on the shelf'." John teased her with a smile.

"I don't believe I'll ever marry," Charlotte answered with an airy wave of her hand, making an announcement of the plan on which she had only recently decided.

"Pardon?" The almost uniform reply of the five people surrounding her, with their accompanying horrified faces and wide eyes, was enough to make her giggle.

"Why ever not?" Oliver asked, his eyebrows so high on his forehead they looked closer to being part of his hairline.

"What else would you do?" John shook his head, apparently baffled by the idea that a woman would choose to remain unmarried.

Charlotte laughed again, enjoying the attention and then the general silence surrounding her.

"I don't need the money or a home, and I don't necessarily think I want children. There isn't any other reason for a woman to marry."

Charlotte had spent several years thinking about marriage, and now that she listed the reasons out loud, she had the clear realisation that it was all true. Her conversation with her mother a few days earlier had merely solidified the idea. She had a yearly annuity on which she could live without her father's help, should the need arise. It was also true that she would have no objection to marrying a man if she cared for one, but she wouldn't be admitting to that. Not openly at least.

"What about love? Companionship?" Oliver wrapped his hand possessively around his wife's waist and pulled her into his side.

Envy ripped through Charlotte, and the feeling wasn't at all pleasant. If she remained a single lady, would this become a frequent occurrence?

"I am blessed with family and friends. Besides, from what I understand from most of my married friends, I'd be giving up a lot more than I would ever gain. If I do still feel a lack of something in my life, there are plenty of orphanages and charities on which I may expend my time and generosity."

Charlotte looked toward a group of young women standing together in the corner of the ballroom. It was well known that all three had husbands who rarely spent a night at home.

"Whatever do you mean that you would be giving up more than you gained?" Sarah asked, her voice rising to a squeak. Sarah was a vicar's daughter who had married a duke. She had gained a lot when she married Oliver, not just emotionally, but financially.

Charlotte laughed out loud and covered her mouth with her fan. Surely Sarah could see the humour in her question?

"I mean, legally, my husband would own me. I would no longer have any control over my money or assets and he, to make matters even worse, would have complete physical access to my person."

Charlotte shuddered and grimaced, then she heard her brother mutter under his breath.

"And you wonder why men keep mistresses?"

"What do you mean?" Charlotte glared at her brother, wanting to stamp her foot on the polished floorboards.

She didn't wonder why men kept mistresses; she already knew. Men were beasts, unable to contain their base urges, but she wasn't going to be the wife waiting at home for her husband to return.

"I mean, if a lady like you dreads going to her husband's bed, why would you assume a husband would want to bed you? He'd prefer the arms of a woman who would welcome him."

Although it was in no way appropriate for Lord John Dunford to be discussing such a thing with his unmarried sister, Charlotte smiled at her brother. She had never been an ordinary lady.

"I'm sure I have no idea what you mean, dear brother. What I intended to say was that he would even have the right to beat me," she replied.

ARCHIE CRINGED at the turn the conversation had taken. Why could his friends never stick to socially acceptable topics? The weather? The gossip? The fashion? He wanted to scream at them.

Pick one of those!

Staring at the birthday girl with an uncomfortable knot in his belly, Archie wondered why she was the only woman who ever made him feel like this. Out of control with his feelings. And a *woman* she was now, not a girl any longer. Tonight was her twenty-second birthday, and Archie had never seen her look lovelier. Dressed in an evening gown of golden silk, with her lovely shoulders bare and the upper swells of her breasts visible, she was the most beautiful woman in the ball room.

Although he didn't like it when her temper was directed at him, he had to admit that she did look amazing when she was flushed with indignation. He suppressed the uncharacteristic urge to chuckle, the ripples inside his belly almost uncomfortable. It had been so long since he'd felt like laughing.

"Well, dear brother, since you have raised the topic, from what my mother and my friends have said, I don't know how any lady could enjoy the bedding business." Charlotte's nose wrinkled in disfavour.

Archie knew that she was spouting a widely known belief that ladies hated the marriage bed, and even fallen women, or women of a lower class, found little pleasure in it. However, he didn't want to add to this inappropriate conversation in any way, so he kept his mouth firmly shut.

"What has Mother said?" John's eyes widened, and his mouth dropped open.

He was apparently shocked that "the conversation" had already come about, as Charlotte had never even been engaged. Archie was surprised himself.

"That I must lay still and try to think of something pleasant so that the time will go quickly. That it will hurt, but it is my wifely duty." Charlotte spat the words out as though they tasted foul. She shuddered, and Archie wanted to groan. He hoped that wasn't what was in store for him.

"Tell me about a lady who enjoys marital relations with her husband so much, she would willingly give up everything that I have?" Charlotte boldly asked their group.

They heard a stifled laugh, and everyone looked toward Rupert. Archie knew that some married ladies enjoyed Rupert's bed, but that was a different story.

Slowly, a small white hand was raised, and Archie's mouth fell open as his gaze met those of the hand's owner.

Charlotte stared at Sarah's raised hand. "You can't possibly be serious."

Her look of disbelief would have been funny, if Archie hadn't been so shocked himself.

Sarah blushed furiously but refused to be cowed by any of them.

"My mother told me that marital relations came down to the husband. If he loves his wife, then he will take the care and the time to make sure that she finds pleasure as well. Maybe that's why so many of your friends hate their marriage beds. They married for reasons other than affection and their husbands do not care for them," Sarah explained. She shot an apologetic look at her now-blushing husband.

Rupert and John looked at Oliver, both with surprised but envious expressions, and Oliver blushed even brighter.

Archie found himself again thinking that Oliver was one lucky sod.

"Well, although I am glad that some ladies enjoy their husband's bed, I am still convinced I will never marry." Charlotte looked sideways at her friend with lowered brows. She obviously wasn't convinced by what Sarah was saying.

"Please tell us, why now, sister dearest?" John persisted, his voice seeming harder, almost angry.

"Because I want things in a man that just don't exist," Charlotte announced to their group, a triumphant grin spreading across her face.

"Such as?" Oliver asked, before her brother could.

"I want everything in a husband, that a man of my class looks for in a wife," she announced, with a raised eyebrow and a flutter of her fan.

"Interesting, a touch backward, but please tell us how that is so impossible."

Oliver rubbed his chin thoughtfully.

Charlotte held up her hands and started ticking off the list on her fingers.

"He must, of course, be a gentleman. He must be of the right age, fair of face, intelligent and preferably someone who has at least as much financially to bring to the marriage as I have."

Archie knew that these criteria were difficult but not unachievable.

"A strong list, but not impossible. What age is the right age?" Oliver asked again, obviously going through the invisible list in his head, considering eligible gentlemen.

"Within fifteen years of my age," Charlotte answered.

"I don't see anything on that list that we can't overcome. What about a title? If you need that, then we might indeed have a problem..." John was speaking now. He had apparently been listening, as he wore a look of intense concentration. Perhaps he also had an internal list of eligible men.

"No, I don't care a whit about a title. I can continue with my own title if need be," Charlotte announced, with a flick of her dainty wrists.

As a duke's daughter, Charlotte was entitled to be addressed as Lady Charlotte for the rest of her life, even if she married someone below her rank or someone with no title.

Archie cleared his throat and leaned forward a little, joining the conversation for the first time.

"Then what is it that you find to be so insurmountable?" he asked her quietly. He could only think of two or three men that would suit her list, but indeed, it wasn't impossible.

"Because I want a husband to stay faithful, and I can think of only one way to ensure that. This particular attribute that I want is the one thing all gentlemen want in a wife, but the wife will never find in a man."

Everyone else in their small circle was so riveted by every word Charlotte spoke that they didn't see the danger. Archie, however, knew her too well, and he was aware that this particular glint in her eye indicated that she was about to drop an unexpected bombshell.

"I want a virgin."

Chapter Four

"No!" Archie exclaimed. He almost exploded where he stood opposite Charlotte, his heart racing as fear set in.

He had been expecting something interesting to come out of her mouth, but not that.

Everyone else in their circle burst out laughing, including Sarah. The sound grated on Archie's nerves so intensely he had to bite down on the inside of his cheek to stop a scream erupting.

He glared at the men who were now looking at him expectantly, their eyebrows raised. Only Rupert wouldn't return his gaze.

Once the laughter died down, Charlotte smiled coolly, fluttering her fan in front of her beautiful face. She looked supremely confident that she had won her argument, and Archie's stomach sank.

"Now you know why I will never marry. My ideal husband just doesn't exist."

Archie knew what was coming and continued to glare at his friends, silently forbidding them from speaking. He saw Oliver open his mouth, but Archie's quelling look soon had him shutting it.

Archie ran through the rest of Charlotte's list, hoping there would be somewhere he was deficient. He was considered handsome, only five years older than her, a gentleman, and his finances were better than most. He couldn't be sure what Charlotte's exact monetary worth was, but her dowry alone would add considerably to any bank balance. Archie glared at his friends again as the realisation began to settle.

Oh God, he was the only man in London who had every trait she wanted in a husband. The idea sent rapid panic racing through his body, his palms sweating as he clasped his hands behind his back.

Rupert was pointedly ignoring Archie's pleading look, as he took Charlotte's elbow and shifted her slightly so she could look directly at him. Archie's breath caught; his heart pounded in his ears as he waited for her reaction. He was about to be unmasked.

"No, your impossible and perfect husband does exist. You're just going to have to marry Archie," Rupert announced with great aplomb and a flourish of his left hand.

The bottom of his world fell away. Without bowing, without a word, without even a thought other than the overwhelming urge to escape, he pivoted on his shining black heels and headed for the balcony.

Charlotte, who was a duke's daughter to her very bones, did the most unladylike thing he had ever seen her do. She ran after him and grabbed him by the elbow, pulling Archie to the side of the ballroom, away from all prying ears.

"What did Rupert mean by that?" She gripped his forearm tighter and stared up at him with intense blue eyes.

Archie stood straighter, trying to ignore the heat of her body pressed up against his.

"This is not an appropriate place to have this conversation." He sidestepped the question and tried to pull away from her grasp, but she sunk her hands deeper into the muscles of his arm.

"Well, where is appropriate then?"

Archie looked at her determined face and angry blue eyes and seriously debated telling her to go to hell. It was none of her business. His hot and hard body had other ideas.

"The garden."

Charlotte's eyes widened instantly.

"When?" she asked breathlessly, her throat working as she swallowed hard.

Archie's eyes narrowed. Lady Charlotte Dunford couldn't be seriously considering meeting him in the garden, unchaperoned. He may have been reckless enough to suggest a private meeting, but she wouldn't be silly enough to agree to it, surely?

"You want to know about my private life that much?" He had spent the last six years keeping his distance from her, and rightly so. Now that she seemed determined to know him better, he felt those long-held shackles falling rapidly away from his body.

"When?" She repeated the question, straightening and stepping back from him as was proper.

They were being watched, and Archie felt the disapproval of society raining down upon them.

"Ten minutes. In the arbour to the right of the garden." Archie dipped his eyes as though he were not interested in what he was saying. But the heat flaring in his cheeks was sure to give him away. At least to her.

Charlotte pasted on one of her society smiles that always made him wince and curtsied as though she was saying goodbye.

"See you soon, my lord." She came back up from her curtsey, and Archie had to strain his ears to hear her words.

He bowed to her automatically as she moved past him, back to his group of watching friends.

He strode off as though he was leaving, heading for the front door as if to ascertain the whereabouts of his coat.

He knew that this was going to change everything, but after being restricted and restrained for so long, he was suddenly filled with excitement. Would he finally be free to express his feelings to the woman he adored? If he did, who knew where that would lead them?

"What did he say?" Rupert asked Charlotte as she returned to their group. He was obviously trying not to laugh, his mouth strangely twisted.

"He said that it was none of my business knowing anything about his personal life. What did you mean by what you said, Rupert?" Charlotte spoke sternly to the known rake of her brother's group.

If Archie did have that sort of secret, it hadn't been Rupert's place to announce it.

"I–" Rupert began, before being cut off by John.

"He shouldn't have said anything. Archie's going to be furious. And rightly so." John looked at Oliver, and they both shared a worried glance.

"But Rupert wasn't serious, was he? I know what you are like with women, John. I assumed all your friends were the same," Charlotte said, addressing her brother.

Again, Rupert started to open his mouth, and Oliver froze him out with his best ducal stare.

"Archie's a bit different than the average gentleman. But that's his business and certainly not a subject for ladies to be discussing. If you'll excuse us, I think we should be getting home to our son," Oliver announced, effectively cutting off Charlotte's questions and any further discussion.

"Yes, and Charlotte, please think about what I said," Sarah pleaded, reaching out to grip hands with Charlotte.

Charlotte smiled at her friend and squeezed her fingers back. Sarah lowered her voice when she came close and added, "And we can discuss this another time if you'd like more information." A lovely blush stained Sarah's cheeks, and she looked up at her husband with transparent adoration.

He flushed slightly and nodded to Charlotte.

"See you tomorrow night, most likely."

Charlotte excused herself as well, saying that she needed to find refreshment. But instead, she made her way slowly out the balcony doors and down the stairs that led to the garden.

Her breathing was irregular, and her heart was beating heavily, as though she had made a mad dash to the gardens, not walked out in as leisurely a manner as she could so as not to raise suspicion.

She had never before been alone with a man to whom she was not related. What had possessed her to agree to meet Archie in the dark, all alone?

She grimaced at herself. Yes, she knew exactly why she had decided. Because she was intrigued by him. A gentleman who was the very last man she would ever have assumed would ensnare her curiosity.

Charlotte caught a flash of movement within the bower and moved toward it. There was only one way to find out more about Archie, and that was to take a step that might lead to the ruination of her reputation.

ARCHIE HELD his breath when he saw Charlotte arrive through the dense screen of trees. She had come alone.

He had no intention of telling her the truth about his family and his brother's horrible secret, but he would tell her a little of what she wanted to know. If she thought him to be a pious saint, he might as well play on that trait.

Charlotte moved covertly over to him, took one last look around to make sure no one was watching her, then stepped into the alcove he occupied.

Their eyes met and he was breathless all over again. He dragged his eyes away but it was an effort.

Archie couldn't remember a time when another person had looked so directly at him. She was trying to find his soul just by looking, it seemed. The air had completely left his lungs. Struggling valiantly not to cough, he inhaled slowly.

"Well, what would you like to know?" he asked, his voice coming out much hoarser than he would have liked. But that's what happened when you had no breath to draw from.

Charlotte bit her lip, her apprehension, or fear, obvious.

Archie clenched his teeth against the bolt of lust that struck him at her innocently seductive gesture. Her eyes were huge pools of liquid blue, shimmering with uncertainty and something else that he couldn't quite identify. His groin was throbbing, his prick starting to swell. With difficulty, he forced his mind back to the topic at hand.

"Charlotte, we can't stay out here long. Ask your questions," he said, perhaps a little too forcefully.

She waited for a moment, then the words burst forth, too loud. "Is it true?"

"Sshh..." Archie reached out for her hand, and he pulled her closer to him, away from the balcony.

Her skin was so warm through her evening gloves, and she was so close, Archie felt his lungs closing up on him again. He took a step back from her, away from her heat.

"Is what true?"

Archie knew what she was asking, of course. He wasn't feeling very gentlemanly at the moment. He wanted to make her ask the question again, to see if she was as embarrassed as he. She looked beautiful when she blushed, and it was such a rare event, he wanted to see if he could make it happen.

She did blush, hotly. All the way from her provocative cleavage up to the roots of her dark hair.

"Is it true that you are a virgin?"

Archie clenched his jaw at the shock of Charlotte's straightforwardness. He considered lying to her, but that would be pointless. Since Rupert had let the truth slip so quickly, he couldn't very well lie his way out of it. Plus, he knew that John would tell her the truth if she nagged him enough. And if anyone could get to the truth by pure persistence, it was Charlotte.

"Yes," he said quietly, adding a slight shrug and consciously relaxing his stance.

He was excellent at expressing nonchalance in every situation. Here, with her, however, he found the posture uncomfortable and perhaps a little stupid.

"How is that possible?" Charlotte spluttered.

"What do you mean, how is that possible? You're unmarried and still a virgin, why shouldn't I be, too?" he asked more hotly than he should have. He knew it was unusual, but good God, she was looking at him as though he were the worst sort of lecher.

"I'm sorry, I didn't mean to insult you." Charlotte reached out her gloved hand and laid it on his arm.

She must have heard his swift intake of breath because she wisely took her hand back again.

"It's just unusual. But why? Really?" Charlotte asked again, looking him straight in the eye.

Archie's quick mind imagined what she was thinking, and he didn't want to draw out the pain. Could he take something away from this?

"What do I get if I tell you the truth, Charlotte?" Archie instantly wished the words back as soon as he had said them.

Why on earth was he voicing his true thoughts for the first time in his life?

He'd spent years lusting after his best friend's younger sister, knowing that he would never have her. But now, she was literally within reach.

Should he kiss her? Would she let him? What would be the ramifications? He couldn't marry her knowing what scandal awaited his family, even if she would have him. She'd refused wealthier, older, more titled men than him. The thought stiffened his resolve.

He reached out his hand and tugged her gently, deeper into the darkened alcove. Tingles of awareness danced up his arm.

"What do you want?"

Her voice sounded husky to his ears, and his body throbbed.

"A kiss," he answered softly. He was closer now, and Charlotte jumped back a little, her eyes huge as she stared at him.

He didn't want to scare her, but there was never going to be a better opportunity to kiss her than right now. Just one touch of those lips before he spent the rest of his life married to someone else.

"Considering your innocence, I wouldn't have thought you would want one." She tried to laugh, but it came out sounding strained.

Archie pulled her closer again. He didn't want her so far away anymore.

He gently pushed her up against the hedge and placed his mouth next to her ear, the hot contact of their bodies making his knees weak. "I won't kiss you unless you tell me I can."

Archie knew he should stop this insanity before it went too far, but he was so sick of his life. Almost ten years of fighting his every impulse. He had kept away from women who could be bought for pleasure, so he didn't contract a disease, and every marriageable lady, so he didn't drag them into his scandalous family.

He burned for Charlotte; he always had. He deserved one minute out of time, but he wouldn't force her.

"Tell me why, and you can kiss me," she said, so softly he would never have heard her if he hadn't been so close.

Archie moaned deep in his throat and raised his hands to encircle Charlotte's tiny waist. Without conscious thought, he leaned forward and told her what his heart had ached to do for years.

"Because, like you, I don't want to share with anyone else. I want a woman who has never known another man. I want a woman who is pure of heart, mind, and body and will only offer myself to her if I can gift her the same."

Charlotte gasped, and her body went rigid under his hands.

"And you've never found anyone who has measured up, apparently."

The petulance in her voice was obvious, and she was doing nothing to disguise it. Where had all Lady Charlotte's infamous natural flirtatious charm gone?

Archie laughed softly against her ear, enjoying the way she trembled when his breath caressed her skin.

Charlotte's knees buckled and Archie's hands gripped her tighter as he used his body to hold her up. She felt so good pressed against him that Archie growled low in his throat and told her the last thing he should have admitted.

"Only one. You."

Chapter Five

Charlotte gasped, and Archie took advantage. He turned his head and closed his lips over hers, taking control, ruthlessly. It had been years since he'd kissed a woman and he had never kissed a lady, but she melted into his arms like the most practiced courtesan.

Archie kissed her with every bit of longing and passion in his soul and felt the very tenuous hold on his control slip away. He ran his tongue along her lips, and when she opened her mouth, he eagerly slipped inside. He slid his tongue along her velvety one, and she shuddered in his arms. He stepped even closer to her, if that was possible, and ran his hands down to her deliciously rounded bottom. Charlotte had always been one step plumper than was fashionable. Archie had always seen it as Charlotte's way of standing out and had at the time dismissed it as another of her vanities. Now, he gloried in it. What a beautiful bottom she had, plump and firm. A real handful on either side for his hands.

Archie's heart was pumping so hard it was almost painful. He wanted her closer. He pulled her into the cradle of his hips, against the hardness of his arousal. That was when she pulled back.

"Archie, stop." Charlotte gasped, pressing her hands against his chest. "Please."

Her whispered "please" cut through the fog of passion surrounding him, sharper than any other tool might have done. He dropped his hands away from her glorious bottom and took two steps back.

His breathing was ragged, and his manhood was straining against his thigh. He used his considerable willpower to pull himself together and rearrange his hair and clothes. In less than a minute he was able to wipe all trace of their encounter from his person.

As long as anyone didn't look too closely at his evening breeches.

"My apologies." He bowed to her, frustrated and aching.

Charlotte took a step forward, closing the large gap between them and reached out a hand to touch his face.

"Please don't."

"*Please don't.* Don't what, Charlotte? Please stop kissing you? Please don't move away? What do you want from me?"

He turned away when he couldn't contain the flickering of emotion moving on his face.

It appeared that this night really could get worse. He had seen heaven, and now he was being dropped into hell. Why had he kissed her? Why did he have to torture himself with a taste of the one thing he could never have?

"Please don't hide from me. I just want to talk to you," Charlotte whispered.

Archie sighed heavily, letting his shoulders drop. Why did he suddenly wish for his dragon back? Why did he prefer the Charlotte he had always blatantly teased for her brashness and her fire? This meek Charlotte just would not do.

Archie spun around in disgust, at her and himself. Mostly at himself.

"Talk? About what, Charlotte? Have you got more embarrassing questions for me? I've revealed enough about myself for tonight, don't you think?

Or do you want to see just how pious I truly am?" He raised a taunting eyebrow at her.

Charlotte's spine straightened as though tugged up by a marionette's string.

"I completely agree, Lord Archibald. Shall we retire to the ballroom?" Putting on her best social smile, she started to walk towards the entrance of the bower.

Archie heard voices enquiring as to her whereabouts, floating down from above on the balcony. He reached out for her, tugging her back into the safety of the bower.

"We can't leave together. If people see that we've been here alone, your reputation would be ruined."

"It would not be ruined. We are allowed to go for a walk in the gardens."

Archie gripped his courage and said what had to be said, a sentence he never thought he'd say. "I cannot marry you, Charlotte."

"I don't believe I asked you to do that," she all but hissed at him, as she spun around, eyes flaring with heat.

Archie took a step back at her anger. He hadn't meant to insult her. He had just intended to explain why it was important that they should not be caught alone together.

"It's not that I wouldn't want to, but–" he didn't even finish his sentence before she jumped in.

"I know, don't worry. You've always made it abundantly clear how unsuitable you think I am. How could I ever live up to the standards you have set for yourself and your future wife?" She was seething with anger now. Archie could sense it coming from her like steam from a boiling pot of water.

With a last scathing stare, she stalked right out into the light to join the women on the balcony.

"Here I am, Mama. I'm so sorry for leaving without telling you where I was going. I had a terrible headache, but the night air seems to have cleared it right up."

"Were you talking to someone, Charlotte?" Archie heard the Duchess of Arrow ask her daughter; suspicion etched in her tone.

"No one," came Charlotte's reply. Then their voices receded as she shepherded her mother and the other dowagers of the *ton* inside.

Archie leaned his forehead into one of the high hedges. How had tonight gone from a typical *ton* engagement to his definition of hell?

Not only did Charlotte now know he was unlike other gentlemen of the *ton*, but he had managed to kiss her senseless and himself too, for that matter, and yes, insult her, all within the space of ten minutes. How could she honestly believe that he didn't think she was good enough for him? She was so far out of his reach as to be laughable.

He loved Charlotte. He had always loved her. She was the epitome of everything he wanted in a woman. Intelligent, outspoken, generous and full of passion. Not to mention, beautiful enough to make every man in England lust after her. But she could not be his, for the mere fact that he had to protect her.

How would she feel if she married him and he got her entangled in his family's scandal, should it ever become common knowledge? He would never do that to her.

So, he had to make sure he never kissed her again. Because the feel of her against him was like nothing he had ever experienced. And it wasn't simply the long-forgotten feeling of a woman pressed against him–it was *her*. It had always been her.

He felt her very presence down to the depths of his soul, and knew that if he ever had the good fortune to know her intimately, he would lose his heart fully and forever.

A FEW MORNINGS after her birthday ball, Charlotte paid a call on Sarah at her new townhouse. Oliver had bought the house for himself and his young wife, and he had given his mother the family's existing townhouse in which to live.

"Charlotte, it is so lovely to see you," Sarah greeted her friend with a genuine smile in the morning sitting room.

"Tea?" she asked, already pouring Charlotte a cup. "Milk?"

Charlotte took a moment to be amazed at how far Sarah had evolved, from the shy, socially inept young woman of a year before. She was now a supremely confident hostess, wife, and a perfect duchess. A credit to her husband's family.

"Yes, but no sugar," Charlotte answered, almost forgetting the question.

She would be happy if she could keep her tea down this morning. She had come to ask Sarah some more questions about her married life, and her stomach was alive with dancing butterflies.

"This house is beautiful, Sarah, but are you sure you would rather live here than in the Lincoln townhouse?" Charlotte took a sip of the fragrant tea, enjoying the heat as it flowed down into her tummy.

Sarah shuddered visibly.

"Yes, I'm very sure. I wanted a house that I could decorate and for which *I* could choose the furniture, without asking someone else's permission."

"You could have leased his mother a separate house."

That would have been the most obvious solution. No one expected Oliver to move to another house. In Charlotte's view, his mother, being the dowager, should have stayed either at their main estate out of town, or leased a small house for herself.

Sarah laughed musically, eating a biscuit whilst she spoke.

"No, Oliver had too many bad family memories there. I wanted somewhere where we could start fresh." Sarah smiled at the butler as he approached.

"Lady Wickersham and Miss Bartlett have called, Your Grace. Shall I tell them you are at home this morning?"

Sarah looked at Charlotte, and her eyes seemed to narrow. Dropping her voice to a whisper, she spoke.

"Are you here to take me up on my offer to tell you more about what my mother said to me?"

Heat flowed into Charlotte's cheeks. Was she that obvious? Before she could even answer, Sarah was sending the other ladies away.

"Please tell anyone else who calls this morning, Peters, that I am not at home."

The butler inclined his head respectfully and bowed, tactfully shutting the door behind him.

"You didn't have to do that, Sarah. I could have called on you at another time." Charlotte apologised profusely. She felt incredibly guilty now.

Sarah waved her hand like the veritable duchess she was.

"No, this is a perfect time. David is asleep, and you are here. There have to be some advantages to being a duchess, other than the prestige."

David. She still couldn't get used to the unusual name that Sarah and Oliver had chosen for their son. Charlotte laughed out loud and found herself wishing she and Sarah had grown up together. What a wonderful friend she would have been.

Charlotte had very few true friends.

"So, what would you like to know?" Sarah continued to sip from her teacup and eat another biscuit.

"I kissed someone the other night," Charlotte blurted out.

She hadn't meant to start the conversation so abruptly, but she had been dying to tell someone ever since it happened. Sarah was the most trustworthy person Charlotte knew. She had no intention, however, of telling her who she had kissed.

"At your birthday ball?" Sarah's eyes narrowed in suspicion.

"Yes, after you left." Charlotte bit into a biscuit before she could share more.

"I won't ask who, just tell me how it was. Was it your first kiss?" Sarah asked, leaning forward in her chair with an excited smile on her face.

"No, it wasn't my first kiss." Charlotte blushed so hotly she reached up and laid her hands against her cheeks to try and cool them down. She was never going to get through the conversation if she was this embarrassed at the start.

"But it was the first time that a man put his tongue in my mouth and the first time that I...ah...wanted to keep kissing." Charlotte stammered over the admission, but got the words out, all the same.

"Did you?" Sarah asked, not showing any revulsion at the idea. Instead, she looked intrigued.

"No. Well, he pulled my body into his, and he had, ah...he was...I got scared."

Now Charlotte truly did run out of words, so she stuffed a piece of cake into her mouth. At this rate, she was going to need to have the dressmaker let out all of her new ball gowns.

"So, he was aroused from the kiss, and you stopped him before he did anything else?" Sarah clarified, chewing her lip thoughtfully.

"Yes."

Charlotte bowed her head slightly, in gratitude. She wasn't sure she could have said it. Her mother and several married friends had explained the mechanics to her, and it sounded horrible.

"So why have you come here, Charlotte? I can tell you anything you want to know, but if you have some specific question, just ask me." Her eyes were bright, and Charlotte saw nothing to indicate that she wouldn't tell the truth.

She took a deep breath and exhaled slowly. If she never married, would that mean she never got to taste the passion that Sarah apparently enjoyed?

"First, I need to know if you were telling the truth, about, you and Oliver...and..." Oh, when had she become such a babbling idiot?

Charlotte had always prided herself on her ability to talk people into circles and out of them again. What was wrong with her?

Sarah laughed softly and leaned back in her chair, a dreamy look on her face.

"Charlotte, can I be completely honest—brutal even?"

"Please. That would be fine."

"If Oliver and I didn't have to leave the bedroom to eat, I'm not sure if I would ever leave."

Charlotte cocked her head to the side. What could she possibly mean by that?

Sarah apparently saw Charlotte's confusion and laughed musically again.

"Let me put that more simply. Oliver gives me so much pleasure in our bed that if we could make love all day and night, I would do it."

Charlotte's jaw dropped. She must have stayed that way too long because Sarah reached over and pushed her chin back up.

"You're serious? It's that good?"

Charlotte couldn't believe what her friend was telling her. It went against everything her mother and her friends had said about marital relations.

"Yes, it is," Sarah assured her, leaning back in her chair again and smiling a secret smile.

"But how? How could a man putting his, you know, inside you, how could that feel right?"

Charlotte was truly confused now. It sounded ridiculous.

It was the first time Sarah blushed, and Charlotte almost laughed.

"When I first heard my mother tell me it could be enjoyable if the man cared enough, I didn't believe her either. Then Oliver kissed me, and touched me, and I suddenly felt an emptiness inside me that needed to be filled. Oliver did that. I ached with hunger, and he knew what to do."

"What did he do?" Charlotte leaned forward in her chair as though she could absorb the necessary information via proximity.

"He kissed me and touched me until I almost died with pleasure."

Sarah blushed again but resolutely kept her head up.

Charlotte considered that. The concept of any pleasure, let alone such a cataclysmic event being possible, was surreal.

"Really?" she asked skeptically.

"You'll know when it happens." Sarah smiled a little smugly.

"Next, I need to know what I can do."

Now that she knew that it could be enjoyable, then maybe there were other things she could do that wouldn't ruin her.

"What do you mean, Charlotte?" Sarah asked, a confused expression passing over her face.

Charlotte blushed again at her audacity to ask such a forward question but didn't back down.

"What can I do to him to give him pleasure, too? If he tries again? Can I do anything that won't lead to me being ruined?"

Charlotte couldn't believe she was asking such things. But she had to know. If Archie wanted to touch her again, could she touch him without losing her virginity?

Sarah blinked once and picked up another biscuit.

Charlotte waited for her to finish and kept her mouth firmly shut, squeezing her hands tightly together in her lap.

Sarah sat chewing for a full minute, obviously deciding whether she would tell Charlotte what she wanted to know. Suddenly she smiled and leaned forward again.

"All right, I'll tell you, but you can't tell anyone that I told you any of this."

"I won't, Sarah, please," Charlotte assured her friend.

She leaned forward in a mirror image of Sarah's enthusiasm. She had the sudden urge to ask for a piece of paper and quill to write everything down but realised that that might seem a little too eager.

"First, my mother told me that anything your husband, or in this case, your lover, can do to you, you can do to him."

"Like what?"

Charlotte didn't understand what else there was to do other than the bedding, which a woman certainly couldn't do to a man.

"Like touching and kissing."

"Where?" Charlotte asked, her eyes widening. Archie had touched her waist and her bottom whilst he was kissing her. Maybe that what Sarah meant.

"Everywhere," Sarah announced confidently, then ruined the effect with a blush.

"Everywhere?"

She couldn't mean everywhere. Sarah nodded, a funny twitch happening at the corner of her mouth as though she were trying not to laugh. Charlotte filed that piece of information away and asked something more specific.

"Tell me what I can do without ruining myself."

"Charlotte, I'm not sure if I should give you information which could get you into trouble." Sarah bit down on her lip, looking hesitant now.

"Look, Sarah, I'm twenty-two years old. I'd never actually, properly, kissed anyone before but I...I have finally met someone I could love. But I need someone to help me. Please."

Even as she spoke the words, shock filled her. *Love?* Archie? Never! Or at least, she didn't think so...

She knew she'd said the right thing when Sarah's face warmed with understanding.

"Well, there are only two ways. You can touch each other with your hands or with your mouths." Sarah subconsciously touched her mouth as though illustrating her point.

"Where?" Charlotte asked, wide-eyed.

"He'll want to touch you here and here," Sarah said, running her hand from her breast to her lap discreetly.

Charlotte swallowed hard, thinking about the times she had touched herself in those places just to see what exactly men found so interesting. It hadn't felt like anything special.

"And I touch him there, too?" Charlotte asked thoughtfully, then Sarah's initial words registered.

"With my mouth?"

She gasped, lifting her hand to cover her mouth. Sarah couldn't be serious. Her friend pulled her lips tightly together and nodded.

"You can, although Oliver told me that most ladies don't," she confided, looking as though she was relieved to finally be able to tell someone that fact.

"But you...?" Charlotte couldn't finish the question. She couldn't even fathom the idea of Sarah, or anyone for that matter, kissing that part of a man.

"When you love someone, Charlotte, it makes you happy to make them happy. Whether that is buying them something they want, or making sure they eat the food they like. This is just part of that love. If you love them, you want to please them."

Sarah hesitated, then obviously decided she needed to say one more thing.

"Charlotte, the most important thing is to listen to your heart. If you're comfortable touching this man, do it. If you want to run, follow your instincts. I learned that early on, and it served me well." Something slightly painful flashed over Sarah's face, then it cleared. Her expression resumed its usual state of general serene happiness.

"Sarah, I don't know how to thank you. If I had listened to my other friends or my mother, I would always have assumed that pleasure was only for fallen women," Charlotte said unthinkingly.

She had been talking about her father's mistress. But then she saw Sarah blanch and realised how that must have sounded.

"Oh, please don't think I meant you. Please, forgive me," Charlotte begged. The woman had been so generous to share her knowledge.

Sarah laughed.

"No, it's fine. I believe you should have all the information. My mother thought that the reason most men of rank are unfaithful to their wives is that their wives don't enjoy bedding. If you want a faithful husband so much that you're willing never to marry, then maybe this information can help you."

"Now, tell me about your beautiful little boy," Charlotte encouraged her friend, happy now to change the subject.

Sarah laughed happily and swept into a lengthy discussion about the joys of being a mother.

Chapter Six

A week later, Archie was still chastising himself for kissing Charlotte. He hadn't been able to get a good night's sleep since, waking hot and erect, with visions of Charlotte naked beneath him.

He should have stayed away from the *ton* balls, where there was a possibility he'd see her again. It was a standard practice of his to attend one ball a fortnight and his club every other day. It was a system to which he had stuck for almost ten years. It made him feel reliable and stable.

For the first time in a decade, he wanted to break the rules. He had seen

Dunford at his club during the day, and his friend had mentioned having to take Charlotte to Lady Marlow's ball that night.

Archie pulled the cord for his valet and took a deep breath. He couldn't wait any longer. He had to see her again.

He may be breaking all of his own rules, but if he didn't, he might never get another good night's sleep.

❧

CHARLOTTE HAD BEEN deep in conversation about this season's hats when an awareness within her prickled and made her sit up straighter.

"Lord Archibald Turner," the butler announced.

Charlotte briefly closed her eyes. How could she be so attuned to him already?

She couldn't stop from turning to watch as Archie entered the room and looked immediately to his left. Her eyes met his. She was drawn to him with a strength that made her stomach tighten.

Archie turned on his heel and headed directly for the card room.

Charlotte clenched her hands into fists in her lap and glared at the back of Archie's retreating figure. She couldn't believe he'd looked directly at her, and turned away, going to one of the male hideaways at such events. Well, if he could ignore her after their kiss, she would do the same.

Charlotte glanced around the room and saw a new debutante surrounded by four gentlemen. She nodded. She could accomplish two things at once. Rescue the poor girl who looked like she was drowning in attention, and also engage her own interests. How else would she keep her mind occupied?

Charlotte sashayed across the room and greeted the beautiful young girl she had met the previous evening. "Miss Bartlett, so lovely to see you," Charlotte said.

"Ah...Lady Charlotte, lovely to see you too," the young lady stammered in reply, touching Charlotte's offered hand.

The young girl looked at her warily, but Charlotte ignored this, taking her by the arm and addressing the men in front of her.

"I hope you gentlemen aren't trying to overwhelm Miss Bartlett," she chided, with a coy smile.

Charlotte recognised all four of the young gentlemen in front of her. Two of them blushed brightly. They were both Charlotte's age and always acted as though they felt vastly inferior to her. The other two gentlemen, however, were Archie's age or a little older and could hold their own in any conversation.

"Lady Charlotte," the older two gentlemen greeted her as one. They bowed grandly, each taking turns to kiss her hand.

"How are you enjoying the evening, Lady Charlotte?" asked the gentleman standing closest to her.

Charlotte searched her memory and came up with a name, the Honourable James Withering, she remembered. He was the heir to Viscount Westleigh. Yes, he would do just fine.

"I'm having a wonderful time, Mr. Withering, although I am feeling a little disappointed." Charlotte sighed dramatically and pouted openly.

"And why is that, my lady?" her prey asked, looking genuinely concerned.

"There has been dancing going on for the last two hours at least and all I have done is watch from the sidelines." She sighed again for emphasis and gave her would-be champion a shy smile.

It was not ladylike to request a dance from a gentleman, but Charlotte knew how to get what she wanted. The simplest way was often just to convince the other person they wanted the same thing as her.

"Well, if you would grant me the honour of being my partner for the next two dances, my lady, I could rectify that problem for you," replied her gentlemen, with an air of benevolence.

He looked more pleased than could be easily described by this most public request.

Looking down at the beautiful young girl beside her, Charlotte shook her head regretfully.

"Thank you so much, sir, but I wouldn't want to abandon Miss Bartlett." Another obvious ploy for a dance, but one that also worked beautifully.

Within seconds, Miss Bartlett had been asked to dance by the other older gentleman and Charlotte was being whisked onto the dance floor. She had to give Mr. Withering credit—she rarely got asked for more than one dance, as that showed intent, but he seemed to have more courage than most gentlemen of the *ton*.

"You look lovely this evening, my lady," Mr. Withering told her, with a courtly twinkle in his eye.

Charlotte smiled warmly. She appreciated the comment whilst the man's eyes were still on her face. Too many times, a gentlemen's eyes hovered lower to her pushed up breasts, and then Charlotte did not dance with him again. Unfortunately, this happened more than half the time, and she would soon be running out of gentlemen with whom to dance. She knew her dress was beautiful and that her body was cleverly displayed, but a little courtesy went a long way.

"So, tell me about your new horse breeding program, Mr. Withering."

Withering looked genuinely surprised that she would know such a thing, let alone ask about it.

"I hadn't realised you had an interest in horses, my lady." Again, he spoke with the perfect combination of surprise and respect in his voice.

Charlotte smiled again, feeling guilty that she was using this kind gentleman just to forget another difficult one.

"I know it's not particularly ladylike, Mr. Withering, but growing up with my two brothers meant that I often had to listen to such talk. I found after some time that it became more interesting than talk of bonnets and ribbons."

Mr. Withering laughed loudly, and Charlotte joined him. She knew that she had a good knack for conversation, but she was still genuinely pleased when a gentleman appreciated what she had to say, rather than what she looked like.

They continued chatting through the next two dances, very easily.

ARCHIE TAPPED his fingers against the wooden table in the card room, wondering if he should leave through the side garden. He could barely restrain himself from going back into the ballroom to see Charlotte.

He had never felt like this before, so out of control. It was as though that one kiss had undone ten years of carefully constructed restraint.

"So, any tips on the latest investments, Archie?" John spoke to him from across the table.

Archie struggled to pull his mind back to the current topic. He noticed that many of the men around him had stopped their conversations to listen. He knew they looked to him because it was well known that he made real money in investing. He hoped that this regard would also hold him in good stead when the family scandal broke.

"At the moment, I'm looking into some shipping companies that have been travelling routes between India and England. But nothing is certain yet, I'll let you know, John," he said, not wanting the whole room to know his latest tip.

John smiled at him and looked back at his cards as Oliver walked in whistling; looking smug and satisfied as always.

"Oliver." Both John and Archie greeted him.

"Lincoln," chorused many of the other men.

Oliver tipped his head to the rest of the room and sat down with his friends. Although Oliver now bore the title of Duke of Lincoln, he wouldn't allow his closest friends to call him anything other than by his given name. It went against the grain for Archie to ignore protocol like that, but he cared about his friend's feelings more.

"Looking happier than normal, Oliver. Any news?"

Oliver leaned forward and pitched his voice low.

"Don't say anything to Sarah, because I'm not meant to say anything yet, but she's *enceinte* again."

"Already?" John asked, apparently surprised. None of them had any siblings within three years of each other, and Oliver's son was only just over four months old.

Oliver blushed and nodded.

Archie laid his cards down with a slow movement and gave Oliver an assessing look. Maybe he should ask Oliver about bedding when the time came. He seemed to keep his wife satisfied enough that she wanted to have his baby again within four months of her first birth.

Strange, but then again Oliver's wife had not been brought up within the *ton*. Perhaps Sarah had been telling the truth when she said that vicars' daughters had different ideas about their marriage bed.

Archie flushed at the thought, and Oliver gave him a quizzical look.

"What are you thinking about now, Archie?"

"Just thinking about how lucky you are, my friend," Archie answered honestly. How could he not?

Oliver chuckled, and John just shook his head.

"Not me. Wives are for men who want only one woman. Couldn't think of anything worse. I'll stay out of the parson's trap, thank you."

John always had a mistress. He never kept one around for more than six months, but he was never without one either. Again, Archie had to fight the strange urge to ask about John's latest bed partner, when Oliver said something that chilled Archie's blood.

"Well, it looks like your sister might have changed her mind, John."

"About?"

John shuffled his cards again. Archie knew he did that when he had a bad hand But the comment about Charlotte had unnerved him enough that he forgot about cards.

"About never getting married. I saw her dance the last two with Withering."

Archie grabbed his port glass and downed what was left in a single gulp, then called for more while the burn made him gasp and grimace. That bloody woman was going to turn him into a drunkard.

Oliver gave him a startled look but went on.

"Not a bad chap. Breeds horses, doesn't gamble much, decent fortune. Although I hear he keeps a long-time mistress in Essex Street."

Essex Street was in a nice part of town and Archie looked at Oliver in surprise and silent question. Reading his look correctly, Oliver explained.

"It usually means that he's in love with his mistress."

John grunted, "Or thinks he is."

"Well, then Charlotte won't marry him," Archie announced.

He was relieved that her strict list of rules would prevent Withering from marrying her. Although his heart was still thumping in his chest and he couldn't seem to calm it down.

"Maybe, although you never know what a man would do for a woman with whom he falls in love."

John grunted again, but Archie's heartbeat tripled in speed. He knew that Oliver was faithful to Sarah, but did that mean any gentleman could change his habits for a woman he loved?

Oliver stood up again, inclining his head.

"I think I'll go and see where Sarah is."

Archie chuckled, the feeling rippling through him and relieving some of the tension in his body.

"You know, you're not meant to care what she does, or to whom she speaks," said John, with a smile.

Oliver smiled back, obviously confident in the knowledge that such men would be unsuccessful. "I know, but I don't want my daughter listening to some rake trying to get my wife into bed."

Archie glanced away from his friend. He was so jealous of the emotion in Oliver's eyes that he felt sick to his stomach with it.

"Daughter?" John picked up on the point that Archie had missed in his green haze.

"Yes. Sarah's decided this one's a girl, and she was right the first time."

"Archie?"

"Yes?" Archie looked at his cards and tried not to let Oliver see the hope he knew would be flaring in his eyes.

"Want to join me?" Oliver asked lightly, but Archie saw the awareness in his friend's eyes. Oliver knew him better than anyone, and he wasn't doing a good job at hiding his eagerness to return to the ballroom.

Archie considered his options for less than two seconds before he stood and followed Oliver. Butterflies fluttered in his belly. Luck was on his side. Oliver's duchess wife, Sarah, was presently talking to both Charlotte and Withering.

Chapter Seven

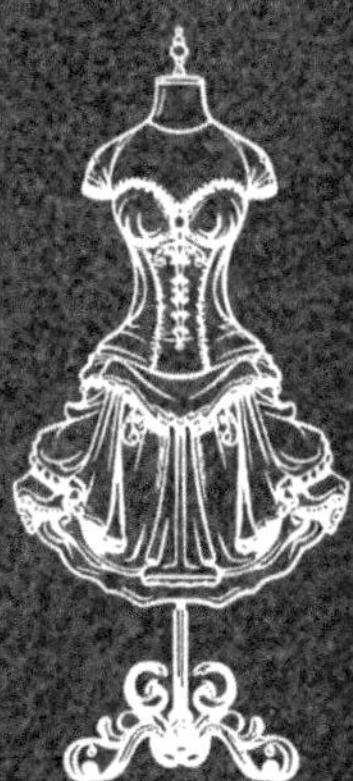

Archie sidled up next to Sarah and tried not to let his face or body show the rather violent feelings he was experiencing. Desire and hatred were warring inside him like a pair of vicious mongrels, fighting for supremacy.

"Withering," Archie greeted the gentleman who had had the courage to partner for two dances with the spectacular Lady Charlotte Dunford.

"Turner."

"How are those fine horses of yours?" Archie knew the Viscount's heir through their mutual love of horseflesh. Withering liked racehorses especially, and Archie could see the passion was high.

Withering laughed and shared a glance with Charlotte. Archie raised an eyebrow and clenched his jaw. What had he missed?

"Lady Charlotte was just asking about the same topic. Perhaps you can tell Turner how my horses are, Lady Charlotte, as you listened so attentively."

Charlotte flushed, her full cheeks turning a bright shade of pink.

"Several of Lord Withering's well-known racehorses have been at stud recently and have produced two young fillies and a colt," she told Archie obligingly, neither smiling nor allowing any warmth into her tone.

Archie inclined his head in thanks but held his tongue. Charlotte turned her back to Archie and spoke directly to Withering.

"What are you planning on doing with the offspring, Mr. Withering? Are you planning to sell them, or keep them to race yourself?"

"I don't keep many horses to run, Lady Charlotte. I either sell them or keep them for breeding. The colt I will keep for breeding. His bloodlines are impeccable, but the two fillies, I will sell."

"Really?" Archie asked, interested now. "What are the horses' bloodlines? I'm looking to increase my breeding program next year."

Archie and Withering got into a discussion about bloodlines until Charlotte spoke into one of the rare silences.

"Are you enjoying the ball, my Lord Archibald?"

Archie glanced at Charlotte and noted the look in her eye. What was she up to?

"I am, thank you, Lady Charlotte," he bowed in acknowledgement, addressing her as formally as he had been addressed.

"Are you going away soon, my lord?" she enquired in a sweet tone. Again, that look was there in her eyes and Archie tensed up for the attack that was sure to come.

"No, my lady, I will not be leaving town until the end of the season." Or unless his brother got worse, he added silently to himself.

"But, my lord, why have you attended three balls in a sennight if you are not going away? I'm sure that in the six years since my coming out, you have never attended two balls in so short a succession."

When their whole group looked at Archie expectantly, Archie could have cursed aloud. How did she even know that?

"I didn't realise you knew so much about my habits, Lady Charlotte," he bit back.

Charlotte didn't even blush.

"Oh, I didn't even think about it until I heard one of the dowagers commenting on it. Then it made me wonder. I don't believe that you have ever been seen at more than one ball a sennight. Is there any reason you are here, especially tonight?" She fluttered her eyelashes and Archie clenched his jaw.

Before he could comment, Withering jumped in.

"We all need to marry at some stage, don't we, Turner?" He grinned, looking at Archie expectantly.

Archie nodded, although he wasn't planning on matrimony in the short-term.

"Oh, is that why you're here tonight, my lord? Are you looking for a wife?" Charlotte asked, and there was steel in her tone now.

Archie allowed himself a lazy smile.

"Well, there are some beautiful new debutantes this year," he agreed, watching Charlotte pale at this acknowledgement of his plans.

It was cruel to make a dig about wanting to marry a debutante, but how could he not, when she was purposefully annoying him?

Oliver cleared his throat as though he was trying not to laugh.

"You're planning on being the next to tie the knot, Archie? I hadn't realised you had met anyone you liked."

Archie smiled lazily again, enjoying the way Charlotte's eyes were sparkling. She would never be a good poker player. Her anger was too clearly written on her face.

"Well, Oliver, I must tell you that the only person I have met recently would be your lovely wife. It was such a shame you took her off the market before anyone else had a chance." He teased as charmingly as he could, giving Sarah his best smile. She leaned forward and hit him smartly with her fan.

Oliver laughed and Sarah *tsked* them both reprovingly.

"You are right, my lord. Who could compare with Sarah?" Charlotte's voice sounded hurt, defeated.

Archie's belly dropped with a painful lurch. He had told the truth, though he had cleverly disguised it. He hadn't met anyone recently he wanted to marry. Because he had met Charlotte many years ago.

Before he could think about what he was doing, he reached out and grabbed Charlotte's arm as she curtsied to leave.

"Charlotte," he pleaded, forgetting to be formal with her.

Her blue eyes flashed at him.

"Don't," she said haughtily. With a sharp move of her elbow, she dislodged his grip and moved to the other side of the room.

"What happened?" Withering asked, oblivious to both the tension and the reason behind it. He didn't even bother hiding his obvious disappointment that his hard-won companion had left so abruptly.

"You shouldn't have said that, Archie," Sarah murmured.

"It was the truth, Sarah."

Archie was unable to drag his eyes away from Charlotte's retreating form.

He heard a small moan of discomfort and turned to see Sarah getting paler by the second.

"Oliver, I know we just got here, but I'm afraid I'm not feeling very well," Sarah told her husband, putting an anxious hand to her stomach.

"Is it the baby?" Oliver asked, the pitch of his voice rising.

Withering took that as his cue to leave and bowed out. Archie knew it was the gentlemanly thing to do, but he couldn't leave his friends.

Lowering her voice to an almost inaudible level, Sarah whispered to her husband.

"Oliver, I think I'm bleeding."

At these words, Oliver immediately swung his wife up into his arms and looked worriedly at Archie.

He jumped to help his friend. "I'll grab the coats, call for your carriage and meet you out the front."

Archie ran off before Oliver could respond, his heart thundering in his ears.

ARCHIE DIDN'T KNOW what to do to help. He had never been so uncomfortable in his life. He was in Oliver and Sarah's carriage facing two people who didn't even seem to remember he was there. Archie had called for a doctor, retrieved their coats and met them in the carriage.

Now he was watching Oliver as he cradled his wife in his lap, wincing every time she moaned as a cramp hit her. Oliver met Archie's eyes in helpless entreaty, and Archie could do nothing. His stomach burned, making him feel sick and impotent.

"I've summoned your doctor, Sarah," Archie told her quietly, breaking the silence.

She lifted pain-drenched eyes up and gave him a brave smile.

"Thank you, Archie, but I don't think they can do anything now." She doubled over again with a moan, obviously in agony.

Archie stared out the window, wishing he had never broken his rule to come to tonight's ball. He shouldn't be here.

When they arrived home, however, Oliver wanted him to stay, and as uncomfortable as he was, Archie was happy to offer the moral support. He was halfheartedly reading a book in the duke's library when a very disheveled and haggard Oliver came in and dropped into a chair.

"She lost the baby." He moaned, dropping his head into his hands in apparent despair.

Archie was again at a complete loss. How did one comfort a friend at a time like this? He reached out and gripped Oliver's shoulder for a moment and then let go. That seemed to do the trick because Oliver sat back and asked for a port.

Archie handed him the glass that had already been prepared and watched his friend gulp down the contents, then reach for the decanter.

"Is she all right?" Archie asked, knowing it was a stupid question, but unable to prevent asking it.

Oliver laughed brokenly.

"She's in pain, but she's handling it well. She told me that her mother had a miscarriage between the births of herself and her sister. And it won't stop her from trying again as soon as we can."

Archie's mouth parted in shock at this obvious lack of common sense. What sort of woman had Oliver married?

"Why would she want to go through this again? We already have David. I think I'll have to investigate some new methods of prevention." Oliver seemed to be talking to himself, but Archie couldn't help listening.

Archie raised an eyebrow but said nothing. Obviously, abstinence wasn't a choice for his friend.

Oliver saw the look on Archie's face and laughed sadly again.

"Don't think it's me, Archie. If I thought I could keep my door locked, I would."

Before Archie had formulated a response to this startling and unbelievable statement, the doctor knocked on the library door.

"Your Grace, your wife is resting. I gave her some laudanum," the doctor announced, with an air of importance.

"Thank you, doctor. Is there anything else we can do?" Oliver asked, wringing his hands in a most undignified way.

"No, but I would suggest not trying again for at least six months," he told Oliver sternly with a hard look in his eyes. Oliver paled but nodded his head.

The doctor's face softened, and he spoke quietly.

"Although, Her Grace did tell me that she wouldn't be waiting that long." With a small smile, he bowed himself out and left Oliver with Archie.

"They all love her, you know," Oliver whispered, sinking into his chair and reaching again for his port.

"Who?"

Archie found himself wondering again why Sarah would want another baby so quickly.

"Sarah. Everyone loves her. The butler, the servants, the doctor, everyone." Oliver's voice trailed off as though he were fighting tears, and Archie felt his own eyes fill.

"I know. We all do," Archie agreed, gripping Oliver's shoulder reassuringly again.

"Archie, I can't lose her...you don't understand...I can't." Oliver moaned, unable to finish what he was trying to say.

Archie was horrified to see tears welling up in Oliver's eyes, and he handed him his port glass again.

"She's not going anywhere, Oliver."

Archie was in completely unfamiliar waters dealing with real feelings. He had dealt with some unusual emotions within his family before, but never this one.

Oliver cleared his throat and drank the port in one gulp.

"I'd better get to bed." Oliver's eyes strayed in the direction of the ceiling and Archie knew he wanted to get back to his wife.

"Of course, I'll see myself out." Archie bowed to his friend, relieved to be leaving, finally.

"Archie, thank you for tonight."

He nodded, shook hands with his friend and walked out the door.

THE NEXT DAY, Archie was standing outside Oliver and Sarah's townhouse again, his hand raised to knock on the door, when a red and flustered Charlotte ran out and almost knocked him over.

"Charlotte." Archie blinked, surprised to see her. He was even more surprised at her flustered appearance. Her face was all blotchy and tear-stained. He'd never seen a woman look as such in public.

Charlotte threw herself into his arms, sobbing.

"Oh, Archie."

Conscious that they could be seen by anyone passing by in the street, he ushered Charlotte back inside and into the front sitting room. The stoic butler looked sympathetic to both Charlotte and Archie's plights. He carefully left the door open and sent a maid for tea.

"It's all right. She's going to get better."

Archie was very conscious of the fact Charlotte was sitting on his lap with her arms wrapped around his neck. His skin tingled where she touched, and heat was pooling inappropriately in his groin. The only thing keeping him from ravishing her on the spot was the fact that she was heaving with sobs.

"It's not fair, it's just not fair," she wailed between tears.

"These things happen, Charlotte," he whispered, kissing the top of her head and letting his eyes close for a moment. He sighed and his body sank into the moment. It felt so good to hold her.

Charlotte hiccupped and shook, and slowly her tears dried up. The moment she realised where she was and who was holding her, her whole body stiffened, and she held her breath. She started to inch herself off his lap with as much dignity as was possible in the situation.

Archie didn't want to let her go but knew he had to.

"I am so sorry," she apologised with an even deeper blush, sliding as far away from him as she could on the chaise lounge.

"Don't be sorry. Just tell me what's wrong."

"What do you mean, what's wrong? You were here last night, weren't you?" She sounded shocked.

"Well, yes," Archie admitted.

"Then you know that she lost a baby. A child who would have been loved and cherished by two people who deeply love each other."

Charlotte seemed irrationally angry, but Archie preferred that over the sobbing.

"I know it's unfair, Charlotte, but Sarah said these things happen."

"You've seen her?" Charlotte gasped, her hand flying to her chest.

"No, but Oliver told me last night that Sarah's mother had also miscarried before."

"Oh." Charlotte sighed, her shoulders sagging.

Archie cocked his head. "What's wrong, Charlotte? You seem more upset about it than Sarah."

Charlotte stared at him for a moment, her blue eyes sad and searching before she finally admitted the truth to him. "I think I'm just jealous that you got to be perfect as always, and I missed out on helping my friend."

Archie chuckled and couldn't resist moving forward and handing Charlotte his handkerchief.

"I'm never perfect, Charlotte. I was just in the right place at the right time to help."

"Withering was there too, and he didn't help," she protested, then flushed.

"He hasn't been friends with Oliver for fifteen years," Archie said, before realising what Charlotte's response apparently said about her feelings toward Withering.

"So, does that mean that you're no longer considering Withering as a potential husband?"

Charlotte sniffed loudly and dabbed at her face.

"I thought I'd made it clear what I need in a gentleman, Archie, and Withering doesn't qualify."

Archie swallowed uncomfortably, a knot appearing in the pit of his stomach. Withering was perfect, except for his mistress. If Charlotte did want someone as untouched as she was, then she would have to marry someone barely over the legal age.

He laughed to cover his tension. "Then I'm afraid you're going to marry someone straight out of school, Charlotte."

She didn't say anything, just looked him directly in the eye with an expression that dared him to say such a foolish thing again.

The air between them crackled with tension and Charlotte leaned forward and pressed her lips to his.

Archie forced himself to stay still and let her kiss him. He refused to deepen the kiss for fear of losing control, but knew she needed some physical comfort from him.

Charlotte must have felt Archie's resistance and cupped his face in her hands to hold him close. She tasted his closed lips with her tongue and moaned in entreaty.

Archie pulled back abruptly, looking toward the door to make sure no one had seen.

Charlotte jumped to her feet in a rush, making an affronted gasping noise. Archie responded just as quickly, getting to his feet in no time.

"Thank you for keeping me company, Lord Archibald, but I think it is time I was getting home."

Archie grimaced inwardly at her use of his formal name. She always did that when she was angry with him.

"You're welcome, Lady Charlotte," Archie replied huskily, moved by the obvious emotion she felt for him.

She may not have known what she felt for him, but it was more than she seemed to feel for everyone else.

Charlotte grimaced and curtsied lower than was necessary, then all but ran from the room.

Archie heard the front door close and quickly readjusted his day breeches. They were not conducive to kissing Charlotte. Even when his mind didn't allow him to respond to her kisses as he wanted to, his body certainly still did. He calculated sums in his head until his body relaxed.

"His Grace is in his study," the butler informed Archie from his usual post, guarding the front door.

The elderly man was keeping his eyes low, and Archie wondered if he had heard or seen what had happened in the sitting room.

Archie struggled to maintain his aloof façade as he walked toward the study. He silently thanked Oliver for hiring discreet servants.

Chapter Eight

A few days later, Archie couldn't believe it, but he was doing it again. He was at a ball for the fourth consecutive week, and there was only one reason for it. Charlotte! He had to see her.

He stood at the side of the ballroom, watching her dance with a Scottish laird to whom someone had introduced him earlier. Nice enough fellow, but he wasn't good enough for Charlotte.

Tonight, she wore an evening gown of apricot silk. The neckline was more discreet than other gowns in which he had seen her, but that only made him want to know what was beneath her dress. He was aware that she would be more beautiful in reality than his imagination could ever hope to create.

As the dance began to slow to a close, Archie decided that it was time to make a move. She wanted him, he wanted her. He didn't know what they could share together, but the time had come to find out.

"Lady Charlotte, may I have the pleasure of this dance?" he requested, bowing to her before she could even leave the dance floor.

She placed her hand in his outstretched one and smiled up at him in an answer. As luck would have it, the band began to play a waltz. Archie swept her into his arms, holding her slightly closer than he should have, but not half as close as he wanted to.

"I've missed you," Archie told her quietly, the only thing he could think of to say. His face showed none of the emotion that sort of statement should have entailed, but he meant the words all the same.

Charlotte missed a step of the waltz and stumbled. If Archie hadn't been holding her quite so close, she would have pulled them both over.

"Really?" Charlotte asked, her eyebrows rising, shock colouring her voice and expression. "Your face doesn't say so."

Archie clenched his teeth and let a little, just a little, of his emotion show on his face.

"I've missed you," he repeated, his voice gravelly now. Some of the emotion he was feeling was obviously reaching his eyes.

Charlotte smiled, a small look of triumph on her face.

"That was slightly better, but you're going to have to work on your expressions."

"Why would I do that, my lady?" Archie asked, swinging her around a couple that was trying to get closer, perhaps to listen in on their conversation.

Archie knew they were attracting attention, but he just couldn't bring himself to care enough to do anything about it. He had known that dancing with a marriageable lady would garner scrutiny, but Charlotte was in a class of her own. Together, it was enough to have Archie wanting to run for the front door.

"So that I can know what you're thinking," Charlotte confided, looking up at him with a mischievous smile.

Archie laughed aloud at that comment and regretted it instantly when he saw even more people look at them with interest. Even though Charlotte was John's younger sister and he was not yet the heir of his family fortunes, the *ton* would still consider their marriage a relatively good match.

Damn.

He stared at his beautiful love for a moment, then slowly shook his head. She could never, ever learn what he was thinking.

"No, my lady, you will never know such a thing," Archie told her calmly, hoping it would always be the case.

"Why ever not, Archie?"

"Because if you knew what was going on inside my head, then you would be running away from me."

"I doubt that very much," she told him, while giving him a smouldering look through her eyelashes.

Archie felt that look as if he had been kicked in the vitals.

"Charlotte, you can't look at me like that, please."

Archie attempted to pull himself together, as though he were a shattered vase. His mask of indifference—where was it?

"Archie, I've missed you too," she whispered, looking up at him and tightening her hold on his shoulder.

Archie had to get her out of the ballroom. She couldn't hide a single thought or feeling, and at the moment, she was looking at him as though she could eat him up.

"Lady Charlotte, would you like to walk along the balcony?" he asked, pulling her to a stop and offering her his arm.

She looked surprised at the sudden change of pace, but took his arm and joined him as they stepped through the large door to the balcony. Cool night air surrounded them.

"Why did you stop us dancing?"

"Because you were looking at me as though I were a dessert you wanted to eat," Archie explained candidly, letting a little of his irritation show when his eyebrows pulled together in a frown.

Charlotte gasped, then a hysterical giggle erupted. She gently dislodged her hand and strolled slowly to the balustrade to look out over the gardens.

"It is a beautiful night, is it not?" she asked.

"Exquisite," Archie responded, not bothering to hide the longing in his voice.

Charlotte turned abruptly and stared at him, her blue eyes shining even in the dim light.

He walked up beside her and propped himself against the balustrade, without touching her. Her breathing sped up, and he watched her breasts rise and fall with such a kick of desire he knew he had to get her somewhere private.

"Charlotte..." Archie began, unsure of how to tell her what he was feeling.

"I spent a lot of time in this house when I was younger. Did you know that, Archie?" she asked airily, waving her hand at the mansion.

Archie turned to her, surprised at the sudden change in conversation.

"No, I didn't, Lady Charlotte." He answered automatically, politely.

"Indeed. Lady Moffat's daughter and I got along well, and we spent a lot of time together here before she married," Charlotte continued, her usually steady voice shaking.

"Indeed." Archie didn't understand where she was going with this but was simply enjoying the sound of her voice.

"And I know of a small room that is both out of the way and has a lock on the door," Charlotte said, conversationally.

Archie's jaw dropped. She couldn't mean what he thought she meant, surely?

"That would indeed be handy for two people if they wanted to be alone," he agreed, leading her to say more. Although he was half terrified of what that would mean for them.

"Indeed, it would, my lord, and I have an absolute yearning to see it."

"A yearning?" Archie repeated, swallowing the lump in his throat and trying to ignore the way his excited heart had picked up its pace.

"Indeed. I believe I will venture to the retiring room for a few minutes and then go visit that place."

Archie debated the intelligence of accepting Charlotte's offer. There was no wisdom in it, only foolhardy bliss.

"Would you tell me where this secret room is, Lady Charlotte?" he asked, tamping down his sensible side.

Charlotte smiled, her eyes sliding away demurely.

"It is through the front sitting room, my lord. You enter the sitting room, and there is a door to the left that enters into a letter writing room. In there."

She smiled brightly, bobbed a curtsey in farewell and headed off the balcony and through the open doors without a backward glance.

Archie stood still for several minutes, his mind a blur of conflicting thoughts. He couldn't do it, surely? If they were compromised, as Oliver and Sarah had been, they would have to marry.

Would that be such a bad thing? His inner self-asked longingly? Yes, it would be. He would be deliriously happy, for a while, and she would become miserable. She would hate him once she found out about his brother, and the scandal that was sure to befall his family. He couldn't abide it. He felt he could bear anything except Charlotte regretting her choice in marrying him.

Archie counted to one hundred slowly and then counted again. He had no choice; he had spent what felt like a lifetime keeping himself apart. Now a decade of yearning was assailing him.

He made his way through the house, watching for people following him and taking steady breaths to calm his racing heart.

He found the front sitting room and walked into it. It was lit by a few candles but was still quite dark. He blinked as his eyes began to adjust, then he saw the door to the left of the fireplace. As he walked over to it, his breathing rate increased and his palms became sweaty. Was Charlotte already in there, waiting for him? The idea made his stomach clench and had him almost running out of the room.

Instead, Archie locked his knees, took a deep breath and opened the door. The room would have been completely dark if it wasn't for a single candle on the writing desk.

"You came." Charlotte's soft voice drifted through the air like misty rain falling on the ground.

Archie groaned at the sound and stepped through the door. His eyes were still adjusting to the light, and he could barely make out her silhouette. He knew, however, that Charlotte could see him.

He turned and closed, then locked the door, before facing her again.

"Come here," he growled, barely able to restrain himself from reaching out to grab her.

She walked into his arms. Archie didn't hesitate. One moment he was standing alone and the next he felt her heat touch him, and he went mad. His lips swooped down, and he pressed hers open, possessively sweeping his tongue through her sweet mouth.

Charlotte moaned loudly at the invasion but instead of pulling away like she had last time, she shifted closer. Archie ran his hands from her waist up to her back, stroking the incredibly soft skin of her shoulders in long strokes.

Charlotte whimpered and ran her hands up under his coat, mimicking the way he was touching her. She tugged at the back of his shirt tails and freed them, running her hands up under his shirt as quickly as possible.

Archie gasped and arched backwards.

How had she done that, and why? He had never felt anything so amazing in his life. The heat of her hands and the softness of her skin against his back was as shocking as dunking his head in an icy pond. His cock was now throbbing painfully and digging into Charlotte's soft belly.

"Charlotte, don't," he urged her, pulling back so that her hands slid away. He moaned at the loss of contact but maintained control and moved to the chaise lounge, sitting down before his legs collapsed from underneath him.

"Why not, Archie?"

Charlotte followed him to the chaise and sat down next to him, reaching for him. Archie groaned when she grabbed both his hands in hers.

Didn't she know how much he wanted her? He had never sunk his cock into a woman's body before, but he could barely restrain himself from laying her down and lifting her skirts.

"Charlotte, you have to know how dangerous this is. I want you, badly. We can't do anything to jeopardise your reputation."

Charlotte smiled her secret smile, and Archie knew he was in trouble. She stood up, slid onto his lap and wrapped her arms around his neck.

Chapter Nine

A rchie deeply inhaled her lavender scent and shuddered as she ran her hands over his chest, sending tingles up his spine.

"Charlotte, I don't know what you want from me. Why are you torturing me?" he asked, letting all the longing seep into his voice. He couldn't resist nuzzling the long column of Charlotte's neck as she bent toward him.

"I want you to touch me, and I want to be allowed to touch you," she whispered into his ear. Archie shuddered as she trailed small kisses across his smooth jawline.

Archie couldn't believe the array of images that now flickered across his passion-infused brain. Visions of breasts and endless inches of skin tortured him. His eyes had now adjusted to the faint light, and he could see her eyes and her face, both glowing brighter than the candle.

"What do you mean, Charlotte?"

She continued to whisper to him. "Sarah said there are ways of touching which wouldn't cause me to lose my virtue."

"There are, but..."

He knew there were other things he could share with her without taking her virginity. All of them would test his control to their limits, but it may be worth it to hold Charlotte this close and touch her intimately.

"I want to touch you, Charlotte, but do you want me to?" Archie asked, running his hand slowly up from her waist and caressing her right breast.

The nipple peaked and stuck out through the thin fabric of the dress. Charlotte gasped and arched into his hand.

Her breath hitched. "Do you know how?"

"Not really. I've heard what other people have said, but I think we're going to have to learn together. You tell me what feels good, and we'll go from there."

Archie chuckled wickedly. Her breasts were so plump and soft. She was so responsive he wasn't sure he was going to be able to touch her intimately and then to stop.

"I can't do that!" She buried her head deeper into the crook of his neck.

Archie grinned and looked down at her flushed face. Now who was being coy?

"Of course, you can. How else am I supposed to please you?" He flicked her tight little nipple with one hand whilst the other slowly reached up beneath her heavy skirts.

She moaned again, low in her throat, and wordlessly parted her thighs for him.

Archie swallowed down the lump in his own throat. She was so trusting, innocent, yet deliciously wanton. How she managed to be all three, he had no idea.

Charlotte clutched tighter onto his neck, the heat of her skin making his body burn. He dipped his head to Charlotte's lips, sealing off the sound of her squeal as he ran his fingertips along her thigh and then inward.

He found soft, damp curls and hot folds of skin. Charlotte clamped her legs together, trapping his hand there and went rigid in his lap.

"Are you well?" he asked, a little more concerned now that he was touching her. Concerned for her and himself.

His erection had just reached some previously unknown limit and was now throbbing in ecstasy and pain. She felt incredible, and he was far too close to spilling his seed.

Archie had heard his friends' jokes about how wet their bed partners became and the lips and petals that lay between a woman's legs. Now he could feel them. Slick with moisture, she was warm and aroused.

"Yes, I... just..." Charlotte tried to get the words out.

"Relax, I promise I won't hurt you." Archie soothed her. He caressed her breast again, stroking the nipple and cupping the fullness gently. *So beautiful.*

Charlotte opened further for him. This allowed him to start stroking over her most private place. He stroked down and found her moistness and upwards where she seemed to be most sensitive. Charlotte moaned and then gasped. He instantly stopped his movements.

"What's wrong?" His stomach leaped up in alarm.

Charlotte shook her head but Archie was frozen.

"Tell me, did I hurt you somehow?" He had no idea what he was doing. She was constructed so differently to anything he'd ever known. Where should he touch her?

"No," she whispered into his ear. "Keep doing that, please?" She arched up into his hand and sighed at the contact.

Archie moaned low in his throat, at her pleasure and her pleading tone. He swept his exploring fingers down and up again. Again, she cried out when he reached the top, but this time, he realised it was a moan of pleasure.

"There?" He found a tiny button within her folds and circled it with his fingers, again and again.

"Yes, there, please, don't stop," Charlotte cried into his ear, her body bowing up into his.

Archie knew that he was watching and feeling the tension of an almost-orgasm. He knew the tension from his past experiences with himself. He wasn't sure how she was experiencing so much pleasure without him being near the entrance to her body, but she was.

As she moaned and started moving her hips, Archie learned what real control was. He could feel the need for release rushing down upon him. Clamping a firm hand down on those desires, he tried to forget about his body and focus on hers.

He moved his fingers away and moved down in search of her opening.

Charlotte arched up to him, opening her legs wider. Archie knew he could put his fingers inside of her but wasn't exactly sure where and how to do that.

"Don't stop Archie, please." Charlotte's voice, husky with need, drove him mad.

"Where are you aching, Charlotte? Tell me, I need to know," Archie begged just as desperately. Where was the place he would put himself if they were engaging in the act?

"Back where you were before," she whispered again, her face burning against his neck, where she tucked it once again.

"Nowhere down here?" he asked, dipping his fingers between her thighs. Instinctively Charlotte opened her legs and pushed against his fingers.

Archie took the hint and pressed two fingers deep into the entrance to her body. His fingers slid in almost effortlessly. Her body was so wet and her muscles so ready, they greedily gripped his fingers and held on.

Charlotte gasped and arched her back but didn't protest as he thrust his fingers in and out of her. She reached for him and dragged his lips back to hers, opening her mouth and welcoming the plunging tongue that mimicked the movement of his fingers below.

Archie knew Charlotte was close to finding her ultimate pleasure, right there on his lap, but had no idea how to push her there. He kept up the rhythm inside of her body, enjoying the sounds she was making and the hot, wet feel of her around his fingers. His mind couldn't help imagining how good she'd feel around his cock and just like that he was horribly aware of his body straining to meet hers. He knew she must be able to feel him beneath her buttocks, even through all the layers of the fabric of her dress.

Charlotte moved on his lap, and he drew back to stare at her.

"Charlotte, you can't do that," he hissed through his teeth. He stopped moving his fingers inside her and could barely concentrate on anything other than her pelvis grinding down onto him and the pleasure throbbing in his balls.

She smiled at him knowingly and asked the obvious question.

"Why not? You like it." She purred like a practiced courtesan.

Archie groaned as he neared the precipice and quickly withdrew his fingers and pushed her away from his cock, further along his thighs.

"You stopped." Charlotte pouted openly. "I don't feel..." She stopped.

"You don't feel, what?" Archie asked.

"Nothing," Charlotte mumbled, ducking her head.

"Finished? Relieved?" Archie asked, knowing exactly how she was feeling, but unlike her, he knew what he needed.

Charlotte lifted her head and looked at him, her eyes wide and so uninhibited.

"Do you want me to keep going?" he asked. Even knowing that there was a possibility that he would finish in his evening breeches if she did.

"Do you know what I need?" she asked quietly.

"Not exactly, but I know where you want to go. I'll try my best to get you there."

Reaching between her thighs again he stopped as one of her hands slid down his chest and softly caressed him over the front of his breeches.

"What about you?" she asked, her voice sounding shy despite her brazen actions.

His cock jerked beneath her touch, all the blood in his body flowing to where her hand lay.

"Don't worry about me; I'll finish myself off later," Archie muttered, breathing rapidly. He attempted to push her hands away.

"I can't touch you, how you're touching me?" Charlotte asked, sliding closer so he couldn't dislodge her easily.

"Of course, you can...but it's probably better that you don't," Archie told her, trying his best to sound serious. It felt so good having her touch him there, he wasn't sure he could make her stop.

"I'd like to touch you, please." Charlotte sounded exactly like herself, and yet completely different. His brazen, fearless Charlotte mixed in with an excited, innocent but inquisitive Charlotte. The combination was lethal.

Archie moaned loudly when she continued to touch him, feather-light pressure over the crown of his aching cock.

"Harder, please." Archie pressed his fingers deeply within her, absorbing her moan as he set up an unforgiving rhythm.

Charlotte arched into his hand and groaned, pushing her hand along his length, matching the frantic pace he set with his fingers.

Archie knew he wasn't going to last much longer. In desperation, he used his thumb to press the small button she had liked him touching previously and was rewarded by a gasp from Charlotte and a tightening of the muscles within her already tight sheath.

They were both panting and kissing and straining against each other. Archie worked his fingers and rotated his thumb, praying for strength as her hands worked their magic on his starved body.

Just when he was sure he would finish before her, Charlotte screamed into his mouth and convulsed in his lap.

Archie sighed and let go himself, his orgasm crashing down on him in a hot, hard wave. He flooded his drawers and groaned loudly. They both convulsed several more times and then slumped together, lips still touching. They were barely kissing yet they breathed the same air. Slowly, they resurfaced.

"What happened?" Charlotte asked.

"We gave each other pleasure," he explained. His eyes were closed, his head still spinning like a top. "Women can experience pleasure, the same as men do, I believe. It's just that not everyone knows to achieve it."

Archie forced his eyes open and took in the beautiful view of her face still flushed from her orgasm. He carefully withdrew his hand from between her thighs and gently pulled the skirts down to cover her legs. She had beautiful legs. Maybe next time she'd let him kiss her in all the places he had just touched with his fingers.

Archie shook his head to dislodge the arousing image. Where had that thought come from? Next time? There couldn't be a next time for them. If he couldn't marry her, *not that she would have him*, he reminded himself, then there had to be no more of these encounters.

If she were compromised, he would have to offer to marry her and then she would hate him for deceiving her. That would be like hell on earth, having Charlotte as his wife, and yet having her despise him. He was literally between a rock and a hard place. He couldn't imagine either scenario working.

"We should go back to the ballroom." Archie gently pushed Charlotte from his lap and stood up next to her.

The wetness in his breeches was cold, and he cringed at the discomfort. He must go home to change instantly. He could not stay in soiled linen; Archie shuddered at the thought. He pulled his jacket together and fastened it at the front, glad the length covered the darkened material.

Charlotte sighed heavily, sounding content. "I can't believe you did that to me with no practice."

Archie struggled to keep the smug grin off his face as he took her hand and placed it on his elbow.

"Well, you had no practice and had no problem with the effect you had on me," he returned as calmly as possible.

Inside he was doing a little jig, but he didn't want her to know that. She had made him the happiest man on earth, but now he had to tell her that this would be the last time they could play with each other, and he was worried how she would take it after what they had just done.

Charlotte laughed musically.

"Perhaps we could meet again next week at Lady Dotherington's ball?" She squeezed his forearm suggestively.

Archie ached to say that he would love nothing more than to repeat tonight's experience, but he knew that getting any more involved with Charlotte would make it so much harder to walk away.

"Perhaps not, Charlotte." He gently patted her hand.

"Why ever not?"

He looked down into her bright blue eyes and knew he was going to have to be harsher than he wished.

"Because we can't be caught, and if we continue to meet like this then, eventually, we will be."

Charlotte sighed as they stepped through the door and moved over to a mirror in the sitting room. She surveyed herself critically in the brighter light. Her immaculate hair was slightly mussed but not completely undone, and her gown was slightly rumpled but not enough to be a problem. Her face, however, could not be shinier or more alive.

"Archie, I am not interested in trying to trap you into marriage. I know that you are probably the only man in London who fits my criteria," Charlotte began, holding up her hand to stall Archie when he opened his mouth to speak,

"However, I also want someone who *wants* to marry me. And clearly, you don't."

Archie swallowed uncomfortably, unable to lie out loud after his senses had been entirely obliterated. He just nodded. God strike him down; he was a fool.

"Good. I enjoyed what we just did, and I would be happy to enjoy something similar again. Please don't turn this into a drama, Archie." Charlotte gave an airy flick of her hand and his stomach dropped with a sickening lurch. Him? Turn this into a drama?

"Charlotte, I didn't mean to suggest that you would trick me into marriage."

"Good," Charlotte said, with an adjustment to her gown and a final critical glance at the mirror. She smiled then. "I believe pleasure agrees with me. My eyes are positively shining." Archie got an uncomfortable feeling in his stomach that he could only identify as fear. What had he started?

"However, you need to be getting home to change. I will see you next week."

Without waiting for a reply she swept out of the room, leaving Archie standing alone.

Why did he feel like he'd been used? He certainly shouldn't feel that way. He'd gotten exactly what he wanted. He'd found his release, and he had gotten his hands on and inside Charlotte. An amazing experience, but one he realised couldn't be repeated. Although he was glad she hadn't turned it into a hugely important thing, he hadn't liked it when she reduced what they'd just done to nothing at all.

Two days later, the question of whether or not to continue intimacies with Charlotte was answered for him. The day Archie had been dreading for ten years had finally arrived. His brother's doctor wrote from their country estate in Dorchester saying that his brother would not survive the week.

Archie had always told all of his acquaintances that his brother was overseas for health reasons. However, that had not been the case. His brother had been brought back to England soon after his illness had been diagnosed and Archie had spent every summer for a decade watching his brother slowly waste away. The physical symptoms were bad enough, but dealing with his brother's mood swings and occasionally vicious attacks were even harder.

Archie took his carriage straight to his parents' residence to join them. They were already waiting in the foyer, packed and impatient to get on the road.

They drove the fifteen miles in complete silence. Not a single tear was shed, and not a single word was spoken during the six hour trip.

There were three of them in the carriage and yet Archie had never felt so alone. His heart ached from sadness, and his muscles ached from the lack of movement.

All he could think about was the outcome of this night. How could they cover up how his brother had died? What would they do if the truth was discovered by others? Archie had always been surprised that his brother's actual illness had never been discovered by the *ton*, but now that death was imminent, people would start asking questions.

He missed Charlotte too, and that made his anguish so much worse. She would have comforted him if she had been aware of what was happening. She would hold him and kiss him and give him that succour he had never experienced, even as a child.

When he was young, about thirteen or fourteen, he had seen the local vicar's wife comfort her son. He had only been a few years younger than Archie, too old for most mothers to bother caring for. He had fallen and scraped his knees whilst running in the village. His mother had come along, dusted him off and held him in her arms until he stopped crying. Then with a smile and a pat on the head, she had sent him off to play again.

Archie had never once had an experience like that. No comfort when he had been sick, no affection when he had been hurt. Now that his brother was dying and he would inherit a title he didn't want, that did not change. There would be no help offered from either of his parents.

They arrived at the estate and ascended the stone stairs. The butler was already there to greet them, bowing his head and opening the door. Archie followed his parents up the staircase. The smell of camphor and other burning herbs assailed Archie's nose, and he felt instantly sick to his stomach.

As they approached his brother's bedroom, Archie held his breath in hope, but the moment he heard his mother's agonized gasp, he knew they were too late. He halted for a mere moment, taking a deep breath to calm the thudding of his heart. Once stable, he moved silently into the room behind his parents and stood slightly to the side of his father so that he could see his brother's body.

No of his parents approached the bed, and Archie felt slightly ashamed of them. The parents who had brought him into this world made no move to touch the man who had been meant to be the next Marquess of Hunting. Their heir, and firstborn son.

Archie's mother choked on a sob and fled from the room, wailing as she moved down the hallway. His father stood a minute longer staring at his lost heir, but then also turned and left.

Archie remained. He sat in the chair next to his brother's bed and said a prayer for his soul. The body left behind was ravaged with the disease. The doctors had told them that he wouldn't last five years and yet he had stayed alive twice that long. He may have died a skeleton, but he had fought to live as long as he could.

Within the week, Archie had organised a small burial, monumentally small. A closed casket, of course, with the church vicar, the doctor, and only their three immediate family members in attendance.

He sent the death notice to the London paper and had the doctor cite chronic lung weakness as the cause. Archie did everything he could do to protect his family, but he still felt helpless.

He couldn't seem to shed a tear, despite his grief.

The next month passed excruciatingly slowly. Archie stayed on at the estate, sorting out tenant issues and paying the bills which his father had neglected. He received dozens of flowers and condolence cards but refused all offers of moral support or visits.

Then Charlotte sent him a note accompanied by a single red rose. It bore a simple message. "Thinking of you."

Finally, he cried.

Chapter Ten

Archie returned to London reluctantly, in full mourning. Knowing they would be unable to attend regular events, nonetheless, his parents wanted to be back in their townhouse.

The day after his return, his worst fears were realised.

"Will you be riding at all today, my lord?" his valet asked that morning.

"No, I believe I'll spend the day in my library," Archie replied, watching his valet adjust his neckcloth and arrange his hair.

It seemed a waste to put so much effort into his appearance when they weren't even receiving visitors, but a gentleman must always look his best.

As his valet was polishing Archie's shoes, Archie looked down and noticed his valet's posture. The normally starched appearance of the proud servant was slumped. What was wrong with the man?

"Jenkins, do you mind my asking you if something is the matter?"

Archie knew very little of his servant's personal life, but he was aware that Jenkins was married with three children and that he was a deeply religious person. Not to mention, amazingly skilled with clothing and fashion choices.

"Oh, nothing, my lord," Jenkins stammered, blushing a dark red.

Archie had known Jenkins for more than fifteen years, and he had never seen the man so ruffled.

"No, really, tell me. If I can help, you know I will," Archie reassured him.

"It's nothing about me, my lord…" Jenkins stuttered again, and Archie let discontent colour his tone.

"Tell me, Jenkins." Archie turned side-on in the mirror, checking for wrinkles in his coat. As usual, there were none.

"No, I beg your pardon sir, I will endeavor to be more cheerful this evening."

Archie wasn't sure that he should let the subject go, but good breeding demanded that he did.

He spent most of the day in the library, reading newspapers and doing research on different stocks. The odd thing today was the servants' behavior. He never usually noticed them, as a good servant should be almost invisible. They did their jobs expertly without ever bothering him. Archie had never felt he was being watched or that he lived in a house with thirty other people but today, he did.

Every maid who came to bring him tea or a meal glanced at him as though he were about to leap on them. They scampered out of the room so quickly he barely had time to say, "thank you." By the time it came around to dressing for dinner, Archie had had enough.

"Jenkins, tell me what is going on. The servants are acting most peculiarly."

"It is not my place, sir," Jenkins replied, helping Archie on with his waistcoat.

"It is, Jenkins. You are my eyes and ears below stairs. Tell me what is going on. Is it the new title? Is everyone worried I am going to close this house up, and they'll be without a job?"

That was the only plausible explanation. This was his bachelor residence, the one reserved for him as the younger son. As the new heir, it would now be possible for him to move into another, larger property.

Jenkins just shook his head, his eyes averted.

Archie turned around and gave Jenkins his best stare.

"Jenkins, you must tell me what is the matter."

"I don't know how to tell you, sir. You know I don't like to report on gossip."

Archie chuckled. His valet loved to gossip, but usually about the *ton*, never about actual domestic matters.

"Jenkins, if there is something I should know about, then please inform me."

"It's about your brother's death, sir." The man stopped work, looking down at the sparkling shoes he was polishing.

Archie swallowed painfully. It couldn't be out already, could it? They had only just arrived.

"Yes?" Archie asked, striving to keep his tone calm.

"I'm afraid that people have been talking about what he died of, my lord."

Archie could have shaken the man to get him to hurry up with his story but held his patience.

"What are they saying?" Archie asked quietly, feeling his stomach drop.

This was the defining moment of his life. Everything was going to fall apart, and all he could do was watch as it crashed around him. Like a vase, knocked over accidentally. You could only look on in horror as it broke into a thousand pieces, never to be the same again.

Jenkins was now bowing his head in obvious shame.

"They are saying he died of the French disease, my lord," he whispered, uttering the words so quietly that Archie thought he might have imagined them.

"And who has been saying this, Jenkins?" Archie asked, horrified to hear his voice so gravelly.

"Most of the servants, sir. I heard it from the kitchen maids, who heard it from the groom of that gentleman who visited your father yesterday."

That was it. Archie had to sit down. Swerving dangerously, Archie lurched toward his bed, landing on the ground beside it with a thump. Pain shot up his spine.

"My lord, are you all right?" Jenkins cried, coming to Archie's side in moments.

"I...we're ruined," Archie gasped out against the pain. His heart was thundering in his ears, and he couldn't slow it down. He had been terrified of this, and yet he was strangely relieved that the waiting was over.

He no longer had to wait for the axe to fall.

It had fallen.

∼

CHARLOTTE WAS WALKING down the hall toward the gardens when she overheard John and Oliver in the library, speaking in hushed tones.

She knocked once and then opened the door without waiting for them to ask her to enter.

"Oliver."

John and Oliver exchanged a worried glance, and then both rose to their feet. Oliver bowed to Charlotte and kissed her extended hand.

"How are you? And how's Sarah?"

"We're both very well, Charlotte. Sarah has missed you. You must come by to visit her again."

Charlotte flushed at the slight criticism in Oliver's words.

It was true that she hadn't been back to see Sarah since that first visit after her friend's miscarriage. It had been over six weeks now. Charlotte wasn't sure if she trusted herself not to confide everything in her friend the second she saw Sarah.

She still felt so raw about Archie's passionate display and then his obvious regret afterwards. It had been five weeks since that night, and she still couldn't come to terms with her vulnerable feelings. She missed Archie so much, and the need to talk about him was a constant physical ache.

"I will, tomorrow. I'm sorry, I didn't like seeing her so unwell," Charlotte admitted, knowing that this was indeed part of the truth, if not the whole truth.

Oliver smiled kindly.

"I know it was difficult seeing her in pain, but she is much better now and is mending beautifully."

They all sat down in chairs around the desk, and Charlotte allowed a smile to cross her face. She knew that teasing Oliver was the easiest way to lighten the mood. However, there seemed to be a tense atmosphere in the study she didn't quite understand.

"It wasn't just that, Oliver. I had to visit her in the ducal bed chamber, and I found it most disconcerting." Charlotte raised her eyebrows briefly.

Oliver's eyes widened, and a deep blush appeared, extending up his neck and onto his handsome face.

"Well, Sarah doesn't believe in separate bedchambers, you see. Her parents only had one bedroom, and she believes it necessary for a good marriage to always be together."

He kept his face impassive, but Charlotte could imagine how much effort that took.

"What do you mean, Oliver?" John asked his friend, apparently confused. "You don't mean, every night, do you?" John's face showed a mixture of horror and jealousy.

Charlotte felt the same. What about monthly times? Sarah couldn't possibly want to share a bed with her husband then?

Oliver shrugged.

"I don't sleep well without her."

Charlotte stared straight at her brother; her shock mirrored in his brown eyes. As far as revealing words went, that sentence floored them both. Their parents had barely shared a bed to procreate. The idea of a duke and duchess sleeping together every night, in the same bed, was so foreign to them as to be laughable.

"What brings you here to see us today?" Charlotte asked Oliver, trying to fill the silence with words.

"Well, I was telling John how concerned I am about Archie. He won't receive me in his home, and he hasn't responded to any of my missives. I know he's in mourning, but he's surely allowed to meet a friend."

A strange, fluttery panic invaded her stomach at the sound of Archie's name. She was sure that everyone could read on her face exactly what had happened between them. It made her feel embarrassed and uncomfortable.

"Of course, he's allowed to accept visitors. He must know that," Charlotte said.

Archie was well known to be the most perfect of gentlemen. He always followed the rules down to the letter. Except, perhaps, with her.

John and Oliver shared another one of those glances and Charlotte felt her blood start to boil. What weren't they saying? If it had something to do with her Archie, then she wanted to know.

Oh, goodness. When had he become *her* Archie?

"Why are you two looking at each other like that? What is going on?"

Looking at their faces again she realised they were keeping something horrible from her.

"Oh my goodness, is Archie sick? Is he dying, too?" She whispered the last words, horror closing down her windpipe; she covered her mouth with her hand.

"Oh, no, no. Nothing like that." Oliver reassured her, reaching out to pat her other hand softly.

Charlotte's heart began beating again. She may have occasionally wished him bodily harm for ignoring her three letters and the flowers she sent over the past month, but she never actually meant it.

"It's just–" John began, then stopped, looking at Oliver for help.

"Oliver, she'll find out soon enough. She may as well hear it from us."

Oliver seemed to weigh these words up before deciding to act on them.

Charlotte felt each second as though it were an hour. Didn't they realise that they were torturing her? That every moment led her to believe something was wrong with Archie, and she bled a little more?

She clamped her hands together in her lap and squeezed her fingers tightly together, a numbness seeping into the muscles, then an ache.

"Charlotte, I'm afraid some new information has become common knowledge, and it is rather damaging to Archie's family name," Oliver explained, telling her the problem and yet frustratingly, not revealing anything.

"What sort of information? About Archie?" Charlotte's mind whirled.

What could people be saying about Archie? He did everything right, everything. He didn't even dabble in those socially acceptable vices that her brother did. Charlotte knew he liked women, so what could have happened?

"No, not about Archie. But now that his brother has died, Archie is his father's heir and will be the next Marquess of Hunting."

Charlotte hadn't thought about that. Would that mean he would be happier to marry her now that he had a title only slightly less prestigious than her father's? Would he take a mistress now? Charlotte clenched her teeth at that thought.

"So?" Charlotte gasped through the pain that her sudden jealousy caused.

"So, there are rumors about his brother's death that will cause problems for Archie." Oliver's jaw was clenched in obvious frustration, a muscle twitching in his cheek.

"What?" Charlotte asked. "People don't think Archie had anything to do with his death, do they?"

"Oh, for God's sake, Oliver, just tell her or she'll be imagining all sorts of crazy things," John almost shouted, obviously as impatient as Charlotte.

Charlotte clamped hard down on her bottom lip to stifle the flow of words.

"Archie's brother is rumoured to have died of syphilis, the French disease." Oliver whispered the words as though it was a great secret.

Charlotte blinked. What did that mean? She'd never heard of it.

Seeing her confusion, Oliver explained further.

"Syphilis is a horrible disease that causes great sickness and the body slowly wastes away."

"Yes…" Charlotte began slowly, trying to see the problem that would cause Archie's family. It was obviously a horrible way to die, but why would that affect him?

"Well, that's horrible for his brother, but what has that got to do with Archie?" Charlotte glanced at her brother and his friend again.

Oliver and John exchanged another one of those looks and Charlotte clenched her hands into fists in her lap to keep from jumping to her feet and hitting one, or both, of them.

"You only get the French disease from bedding whores," John told her quietly. "Dirty whores."

Charlotte was her mother's daughter and instantly saw the social ramifications this would cause. Archie would be tainted by association. Even if he were clean and healthy, the whole of society would now assume the entire family to be diseased and unclean.

Oh, my poor love.

"Archie won't agree to see you?" she asked, sitting up straighter in her chair. She was calm now, a plan forming in her head.

Archie needed her, and if that meant she went to his home unchaperoned and had to push past the butler to get in, she would do it. She wasn't the daughter of a Grande Dame for nothing.

Oliver eyed her warily. "No, he won't see us. He's probably worried that we'll either spurn him, or he's trying to protect us. Knowing Archie, it's probably the latter."

Oliver sighed and took a sip of the brandy in front of him.

"Is he still at his bachelor lodgings?" Charlotte asked.

John looked worried now, his eyebrows rising high on his forehead. "Yes, why?"

"I just wanted to send him some flowers and my condolences," Charlotte told them both coolly, standing up to flick her skirts into perfect folds with practiced ease.

"I will see you soon, Oliver. Give my love to Sarah." Charlotte nodded her head and swept out of the room.

Chapter Eleven

She calmly walked up the stairs and called for her maid. Changing into her darkest day dress in a navy blue, she readied herself for her confrontation with Archie. If her brother was right, then Archie would not want her anywhere near him or his house. He would be afraid to taint her with the brush with which he was being painted. Well, she just didn't care.

If people saw her enter his house alone, then she was ruined. Somehow, she couldn't dredge up the necessary horror at this idea. She never meant to marry if she couldn't have Archie, so what would it matter if she became "unmarriageable?" Even so, for Archie's sake, she would go at five o'clock in the evening. No one would be around. Everyone would be at home preparing for dinner or an event in the evening.

Dismissing her maid, she made her way down the stairs.

"I need the carriage, Stevens," Charlotte told their butler.

"Of course, Lady Charlotte. May I call for Lizzie?" He snapped his fingers, and a footman appeared next to him.

"No. I already have her doing something for me. I only require the small carriage, Stevens. I need to get out of the house and feel like seeing the park. I will be back within the hour. I won't be stopping anywhere."

She marvelled at how well she could lie when she had to.

The butler seemed slightly disturbed by this announcement but showed no other signs of disapproval.

Charlotte was within the confines of the small, unmarked carriage within ten minutes, her heart beating like a drum against her ribcage and her belly fluttering with nerves of every kind.

～

ARCHIE WAS SITTING in his library when he heard a knock at the door.

"Lady Charlotte Dunford, my lord," Archie's butler announced, his usually solemn voice even lower today.

"No," Archie almost shouted at Hill.

She couldn't be here; she shouldn't. Even as he thought up the words to negate his butler's decree, she glided into the room and stood to face him.

"Please ask Lady Charlotte to come back another time, would you, Hill?" Archie asked his butler, ignoring the angry look Charlotte shot him from over the butler's shoulder. His palms began to sweat, and a lump lodged itself in his throat.

"Thank you, Hill." Charlotte dismissed the man instead, giving Archie's old butler a reproving stare as she hustled him out the door and shut it firmly behind him.

Whirling around in a flurry of skirts, Charlotte looked like an avenging angel as she faced him.

"How dare you try to send me away!" she hissed, her hands clenched at her sides.

"Did anyone see you arrive?" Archie ignored her angry words and stood up, his legs shaking beneath him. "Maybe we can sneak you out through the servant's entrance, and no one will see you leave."

Charlotte ignored his words and sat down in the chair opposite his desk.

She arranged herself appropriately, her face a mask of politeness as she gestured to his chair.

"Please sit down, my lord."

Charlotte's tone left no room for discussion and Archie had to quell the instant reaction of wanting to drop instantly into the chair opposite her.

Archie had no idea what she wanted but sitting down and discussing it would not be in his best interest. Or hers. She had a way of making him forget everything but her, and in his current state of melancholy, that was far too tempting a proposition.

"Lady Charlotte, I don't think you should be here. Perhaps I could call on you at your parents' residence?" He was imploring, still continuing to stand whilst she sat.

He had no intention of calling on her ever again of course, but he had to say something to get her out of his house. His bachelor household, for goodness' sake!

When she continued to gaze at him, he tried again. "You know very well that you shouldn't have called on me here. Unchaperoned, too." She knew every rule inside out and back to front. This meeting broke so many rules he was beginning to feel dizzy.

"Oh, pish posh," Charlotte said, as she waved her hand. "Are you expecting many visitors?" She quirked an eyebrow in an ironic question.

Archie sat down in his chair with a thump, the leather soft beneath his hands.

"You know, then."

It was no worse than he feared, but he had somehow hoped she wouldn't find out.

"About your brother? Of course, I know. My deepest condolences to you, Archie. Didn't you receive my notes?" Her eyes softened, and Archie wanted to kiss her.

No one had bothered to express their sorrow at the loss of his brother since his manner of death had become known. They were too busy talking about the scandal of his death. Why he had died. Archie had known it would be useless to try and hide the truth, and it had been. People always found out.

"Thank you, Charlotte," Archie whispered. "But you really must go."

"Why? I need to speak to you."

"If you are found in here with me, alone..." Archie began, but Charlotte cut him short.

"I know. I'd have to marry you. But since you have decreed, several times, that you don't want to marry me, I suppose I'd just be ruined."

Archie's mouth dropped open. She had believed him when he said he didn't want to marry her? Oh, God, if only that were the truth. He would give up his fortune, his new title, anything he could give up to marry Charlotte. But how could he? When his name was now ruined as he had always known it would be?

"I would never let you be ruined, Charlotte," he murmured.

"Better that, than be married for life to a man who didn't want me," Charlotte said spitefully, her eyes flashing at him.

"Of course, I bloody want you!" Archie shouted, without thought.

Charlotte gasped, her eyes wide.

"You know I want you, Charlotte, I have proved that time and time again, but as I have told you before, I cannot marry you." Archie knew he was being cruel, but the truth poured out of him along with his anger.

Charlotte stood up and walked to the back of the room.

"Cannot," she repeated then turned around to face him, her eyes shimmering with tears. "Or will not?"

"Charlotte, must you make me say it? My name, my family's name is now completely ruined. I could never drag you into what we have become. We will be lucky if polite society even accepts us after our mourning period has finished." He raked a hand through his already disheveled hair.

"You've known about your brother's illness for a long time, haven't you?" she asked quietly.

Archie didn't know what he had expected next from Charlotte, but that wasn't it. He was emotionally wrung out and had no strength to lie to her.

"Yes, my father told me the week before my eighteenth birthday," he admitted, dropping into his study chair without waiting for her to sit also.

"And that is the reason you have never visited a brothel before?" Charlotte prodded gently again.

Archie laughed a little bitterly. Everything Charlotte believed about him was about to be dragged through the mud.

"Yes, it is. My father told me to keep myself alive and out of the whorehouses. You've always told me I was self-righteous, but the truth is I was just too scared. Isn't it funny? I'm not any better than all of those men you despise for having mistresses, because if it weren't for my father, I would be the same."

"Why didn't you find a lowborn virgin and make her your mistress? You could have bedded her as much as you wanted and you wouldn't have risked a disease."

Archie stared at the woman opposite him. He was shocked by the fact that Charlotte had come up with this obvious solution because it had been one he had considered many times before.

"I couldn't afford a mistress," Archie countered.

Charlotte made an unladylike snorting noise.

"It's true. You have to pay for rent on a house, clothes, servants, jewels..." He realised too late his mistake and shut his mouth quickly.

"So, you had considered it?" she asked, still quiet.

"Yes, I had," he admitted, "I told you I was just as bad as any other gentleman."

Charlotte moved around him and placed her hands on either side of his face. He refused to look at her, obviously mortified. She moved again so that she was sitting on his desk in front of him and caressed his cheeks with her bare hands.

"It isn't what we wish we could do that makes us who we are. It's what we do that's important."

She exerted pressure on his jaw and after a moment, Archie let her have her way.

Raising his head, he looked into her eyes. Charlotte studied his face for long moments before she pressed her lips to Archie's and slid her arms around his neck.

Archie allowed the kiss because it felt so damn good to have her in his arms again, but he had every intention of stepping away from her once she'd finished. It wasn't until her tongue stole into his mouth and her body pressed against his as she slipped into his lap that his resolve disappeared.

He ravaged her mouth with all the pent-up longing in his soul. He loved this woman. He loved her heart, he loved her sense of humour, he loved the fact that she had come to his home to offer support despite the scandal. He ran his hands down her back, enjoying her small frame, grabbed her fleshy bottom with both hands and pulled her fiercely closer to his aroused body.

She moaned loudly and renewed her attack on his mouth.

Archie broke away, gasping, and pulled them both into a standing position so that he could get away from her. He turned his back, trying to control his body, which was shuddering with desire. He could lay her down right here in the study, and no one would know.

"Archie, please," Charlotte begged, pressing her body against his back and sliding her hands around his waist. Her persistence was confusing.

"Charlotte, what do you want?" Archie turned around, letting his anger get the better of him. "Tell me, please. I will give you anything you want, but do not make me wish I was a different person. Please, you are killing me."

This admission almost tore his heart out, but Archie couldn't bear her being so understanding, touching him, kissing him. If he couldn't marry her, then he couldn't have her at all.

"I..." Charlotte stammered.

"Charlotte, tell me what you want from me!" Archie was seconds away from walking out the door and not coming back.

"You," she whispered. Archie's heart skipped a beat. "I...want you." She repeated, a little louder.

"You're going to have to be more specific," Archie growled. She couldn't mean what he thought she meant.

"I want you to make love to me. Here. Now."

Archie was so stunned he could have been pushed over by a feather.

"But...you know I can't marry you." It hurt to say the words, but Archie made himself say them.

Charlotte blinked and set her jaw. Never a good sign.

"I want you," she repeated, and she pushed his jacket off his shoulders and roughly pulled his shirt out of his breeches.

Archie didn't know if he was dreaming, but for the first time in his life, heaven was being offered to him at the time when he most desperately needed it.

"Charlotte, we shouldn't..." He made one last attempt at a denial and Charlotte ran her hand lightly over the front of his breeches. Her touch burned through the material, igniting him in a way that he had never experienced before.

With a muttered curse that included a deity, Archie launched himself at her and began kissing her passionately, forcing her lips open with his own and stroking her tongue with his. Over and over again. His mind raced with every small bit of sexual information he had ever heard. He knew that sex for the first time hurt most women and with his lack of experience, he wasn't sure he could be as gentle as she needed him to be.

He broke away from her again, groaning with the effort it took to do so.

"Charlotte, you know I've never done this before. What if I hurt you? What if I don't give you enough pleasure?" His tone was anxious as he slid his hands up and down her back.

There would be nothing worse than that for him.

CHARLOTTE SMILED AT *HER* ARCHIE. She felt as if he was hers, all the way down to her soul. She knew she'd made the right decision today, because she loved this man with all of her heart.

Which other gentleman would still be trying to talk her out of this? And whom else would worry that he couldn't please the woman he was with? From what her married friends other than Sarah had told her, their husbands walked in, lay on top of them and then left.

Instead of dreading what was to come, Charlotte wanted to rip all of Archie's clothes off and beg him to take her.

"We'll learn together," she whispered, against his full lips.

She stroked down his chest and circled his nipples with her fingertips. They grew hard and stood out against his shirt and his breath hissed out between his teeth. Charlotte could hear Sarah's voice in her head telling her that there was more to lovemaking than just the bedding. You could touch and kiss every part of a man's body. Charlotte blushed at the thought, but that didn't stop her from untying the laces on his shirt with shaking fingers.

Archie stood there like a statue, breathing hard and clenching his fists on both sides. It gave Charlotte an incredible feeling of feminine power that she could reduce this controlled, virtuous man to a bundle of fire and nerves. She finished unlacing his shirt and pushed the garment off his shoulders.

Charlotte sucked in a breath and ran her hands lovingly over the muscles clenched in Archie's chest and arms. He was wiry and lean. Charlotte knew that he liked to work with horses and ride, but she hadn't realised that would make his body so beautiful.

"Touch me, please..." Archie begged her.

"I am," Charlotte half-giggled.

"Down here," he whispered, indicating the burgeoning flesh between his legs. "I need you to bring me to my release like you did that night at Lady Moffat's. I'll never last otherwise."

Charlotte smiled eagerly and ran her hands down the lean muscles of his chest.

Archie's lips spread open, giving her a wolf-like smile, all dangerous teeth as he opened his breeches. He guided her hand inside, and she wrapped her fingers around his already hard and hot staff. He groaned as she squeezed him and reached for the ties on her bodice with trembling hands.

Charlotte was in awe. What a scary and amazing thing for a man to possess. The skin was the softest she had ever felt, and yet it was solid and hard beneath the silky-smooth skin. She tentatively stroked him, around the bulbous head and up and down the shaft.

Archie moaned and pushed the material of her bodice down to expose both of her breasts. They popped out with a bounce, and she gasped as he curved his fingers around the flesh of one.

Charlotte bit her lip as heat unfurled in her belly. "I thought I was just touching you."

Archie laughed hoarsely. "Touching you arouses me."

He bent his head and sucked one of her aching nipples into his mouth.

Charlotte groaned and arched her back so that he would suck harder. She let go of his hard flesh and threaded both of her hands into his hair, holding his head to her breast.

Archie sucked both of her breasts one after the other, pulling back so that he could turn her around and finish undoing her laces.

"You are driving me crazy, Charlotte; I will never be able to pleasure you properly."

He yanked at the laces and Charlotte smiled at his need for her. This was exactly what she wanted.

"You have already given me more pleasure than you know."

"No, back to my original plan."

Charlotte frowned, her mind fuddled; what was that plan? He grabbed her hand and guided it back to his manhood. He wrapped her fingers around the thick shaft and made her stroke him tightly. Charlotte adjusted her grip to something mimicking his.

"Stroke me like this until I come," he choked out as she began to move her hand in the way he had just taught her.

"Come?" she asked, not understanding what he meant.

She was starting to breathe heavily. There was something very arousing about the pleasurable noises he was making and the flush in his face.

"Find my release."

"And you'll be able to find it again with me, later?" Charlotte asked, frowning. It suddenly occurred to her that he was trying to stop their love-making early.

"Trust me."

So, Charlotte pulled at his flesh the way he had taught her and within moments he was moaning and thrusting into her hand. He swooped down for one long kiss and groaned low in his throat. Charlotte kissed him back, then his body jerked in her arms and a warm fluid covered her hands and the shirt he held to his front.

Charlotte pulled back and watched with fascination as Archie's face filled with blood, his eyes closed in what appeared to be pain. Then he sighed and opened his eyes. The last time this had happened, Charlotte had been too caught up in her own orgasm to watch Archie's face. This time, she did, and it was a revelation.

"Your turn," Archie growled, wiping her sticky hand with the shirt and impatiently tossing it across the room.

Charlotte squealed when he picked her up into his arms and walked a couple of steps to the chaise lounge against the wall. He lay her down gently then stood back to stare down at her.

"Charlotte, if you want to stop, now is the time to say so."

Love blossomed through her like the wild ivy that grew around their house, thriving despite the gardener's attempts to control it. Charlotte swallowed the fear down, her stomach clenching almost painfully. She pushed her chemise and drawers down her hips and onto the floor, shivering despite the warmth of the room.

Chapter Twelve

Laying back again, she didn't move to cover herself like every instinct was screaming at her to do. There were a dozen candles lit in the room, and he could see every inch of her. What if he thought her ugly?

Archie swallowed, his eyes running the length of her body. Charlotte flushed at his perusal, embarrassed by the slick heat gathering between her thighs. She needed this man so much.

She held out her arms and Archie knelt down next to her and kissed her with his tender, soft lips. First, on the forehead and then on the eyelids, his hot breath moving over her skin. He made his way slowly down her trembling body, licking her with his wet, smooth tongue, her collarbones, her ribs, her navel.

Charlotte had never imagined that being kissed and fondled like this would feel so amazing. Everything he did made her want to cry out in pleasure and every once in a while, a lick of fire would find its way to that place between her thighs, and she would push her legs together to try and hide the evidence. She didn't know what to do with her hands, so she just pushed them down into the soft material of the chaise.

Archie ran his lips down to the curls at the apex of her thighs and flicked his tongue out to taste her there. Charlotte sat up and went to push Archie away. She couldn't believe he was about to kiss her there. He couldn't— anything else, but not there.

"Archie, you shouldn't..." she began and stopped.

He looked up and gave her one of those smouldering, "I want you" looks that she was starting to love.

"Trust me," he repeated, for the second time that night.

He moved to the end of the chaise so that he was kneeling directly between her legs and pulled her gently closer to the edge so that her legs hung over the side.

Charlotte covered her face in mortification. He was looking at her in a place Charlotte, herself, had never even seen.

"You are so beautiful, my Charlotte," he whispered, stroking the inside of her thighs and exploring her with his fingers.

She shuddered in response to his words, as well as his touches.

"You are mine, aren't you, Charlotte?" Archie asked as he slid his middle finger deep inside her already wet body.

"Yes," she moaned, mindless with need as she arched her back high.

Archie moved his finger inside her in a prelude to what was still to come. In and out, in and out, adding a second finger, stretching her body.

"Mine, tonight," he insisted.

Charlotte looked down at his fingers moving inside her, his head lowering to her flesh again.

It was time he knew the truth. "Not just tonight. Always."

Archie's eyes widened for a moment, and his fingers faltered in their movement. Then he fastened his mouth to her core, sucking and licking her over and over. And this time she didn't push him away. She couldn't. The heat built and consumed her, the flames licking her body as Archie's tongue drove her higher and higher, until she felt her orgasm roar down on her.

"Yes, Archie, yes!" she screamed as her belly tightened and the coiled spring released, sending shockwaves of pleasure along every nerve. She could feel Archie's fingers still moving as he pushed her over the hill and beyond.

Charlotte shuddered as Archie moaned against her flesh and gave her one more lick.

"Ahhh..." She cried out as he removed his fingers and got to his feet.

Her orgasm had been so powerful that tiny tingles of pleasure were still running along her limbs. She heard Archie divest himself of the remainder of his clothes, but couldn't bring herself to open her eyes.

"Charlotte, come join me." Archie's words broke through her haze as he pulled at her hand.

She forced her eyes open to see Archie lying on his side on the floor. There, between his legs was a huge pole, pointing toward her. Or so it seemed. He was enormous.

Oh, damn!

Having come this far, Charlotte decided that she would have to trust him not to kill her. She slid awkwardly off the lounge, landing beside him with a thump. Archie rolled instantly on top of her, and Charlotte clamped her legs together. The feel of his body completely naked against hers felt wonderful, but the fear of what he was about to do drove all other thoughts out of her head.

Archie smiled, but his expression was strained. Charlotte began to panic.

"Archie, I don't know if this is going to work. You're too big to fit inside me. I'm sure you'll kill me..."

"It'll be all right, Charlotte," he reassured her, with another tight smile.

"How do you know? You've never done this before. You could be much larger than most men."

"Just trust me," he whispered for the third time that night, dropping a kiss onto her nose. "You know, it could hurt you to start with."

Charlotte nodded. She had heard different accounts of the pain accompanied with penetration. She only hoped she experienced the lighter version of it.

"Kiss me again," she urged him, desperate to forget her worries and get back to the pleasure-drugged haze she had been in moments before.

Archie kissed her as though he wanted to devour her and she returned the kiss with equal fervour. He touched her breasts and belly, stroking the place between her legs until she thought she would go crazy with need once again.

Charlotte lifted her hips in silent invitation, and Archie took it.

Lifting himself up on his forearms Archie moved until the head of his staff was nudging her wet entrance. She gasped at the feel of it, and he caught her lips in another kiss and pressed forward.

Charlotte felt an overwhelming urge to push him off as he slid part of the way inside. This was just plain uncomfortable. He was fitting, somehow, inside of her, but it felt like the pressure would kill her. It was not painful exactly, but he was stretching tissues that had never stretched before, and the sensation was not pleasant.

"You know I have to…" Archie said, stilling within her.

"Just do it!" she cried, hoping this part would pass quickly.

Archie thrust hard, burying himself completely inside her. The sharp pain flashed, almost tearing Charlotte in two, or so she feared. Then just as quickly, it was gone. She lay still, listening to Archie tell her how beautiful she was, and feeling disappointed that her mother was right. This part she wished would be over as quickly as possible. She felt uncomfortable with her legs on either side of him, pushed apart, so she raised her knees and wrapped her legs around his hips, relieving some of the stiffness within her.

Charlotte bit back a moan as Archie arched his back and a delicious feeling sparked inside her. Different from the pleasure he had given her with his mouth. Deeper, more intense. Charlotte pushed up against him, and he pulled back and thrust into her again with more power. She gasped and wriggled. That was better.

He began moving with a rhythm, slowly at first, sliding in and out of her. It was quite odd really. Then he began to move faster, pounding into her harder and harder, and somehow she knew to squeeze her inner muscles, pushing them closer to their goal.

He pulled back onto his knees and brought her hips with him. This seemed to allow him to thrust easier, and Charlotte could look at his face better, which she loved. She could tell her own face was flushed and her breasts bounced in time with his thrusts which. all-in-all, was quite vulgar.

His eyes took all of this in while she watched his flat belly ripple and his eyes get ever darker with his arousal.

"Come with me, Charlotte. Now, please."

Charlotte saw the man she loved towering over her, begging with words and with his body for her to go with him, wherever he was going. It was happening again. Her body was tightening, the pleasure building to that crescendo.

With his final lunge and roar, Archie's flesh spasmed within her, and the warm pulse of his seed pushed her over that invisible edge, and she cried out, shuddering in his arms as he collapsed on top of her.

~

ARCHIE COULDN'T BELIEVE it had been so good. He had always known that once he felt a woman's body around him, he would never be able to go back. No, not just any woman. *Charlotte's* body. It was one of the reasons he had abstained for so long.

He knew what he had been missing now. He slowly disengaged and lay beside her, both of them still panting from their exertions. He had felt her convulse around him just as his world exploded and that had given him a satisfaction almost equal to the one she had earlier provided for him.

"Are you all right?" he asked, propping up his head on one hand.

Charlotte smiled one of her brilliant smiles as she turned her head to look at him.

"That was incredible," she answered. Then she reached for her chemise and pulled it over her head and down her body, covering her lush curves.

"Oh. I'm sorry. I think I've ruined your jacket."

Looking down to the spot Charlotte indicated, he saw the blood. Archie swallowed hard.

"I'm the one who should be sorry, Charlotte. I just took something from you which I had no right to take."

Regret and guilt were coming in hard, and Archie was drowning in it. His chest was tight, and he couldn't breathe properly.

"I wanted to give myself to you. I don't regret it," she said, and thrust her chin up, which forced him to look at her. "Do you?"

"Do I regret the most beautiful experience of my life? I can't," he answered honestly, some of the nerves settling in his belly on seeing her happiness.

"Good," she said, curling into his side.

Archie held her, wishing they were elsewhere. Alone in his bed, married, and somewhere that no one knew who his family were or what he was. He may have been the heir to the Marquess of Hunting, but it was now a title ruined with scandal.

"Charlotte, we have to get you home before anyone realises where you've been." Or what you've done, Archie finished in his head.

Charlotte stood up on wobbly legs and began dressing again.

"I don't care if people know I've been here. I'm not ashamed of loving you," Charlotte announced to the quiet room with all the fire she had always possessed.

Archie sighed. He should have expected this, and God, he loved her for her passion.

"Charlotte, I won't have your name ruined by your association with me."

"I'm already ruined, Archie. I've never wanted anyone but you, so what does it matter if the world knows it?"

"What? Do you think I'll allow people to call you a whore?" Archie jumped to his feet with a start, horrified that she would suggest such a thing. He pulled his breeches on, his sticky body uncomfortable and aching.

Charlotte faced him squarely, hands on her abundant hips.

"I didn't mean that," she shouted back. "And I wouldn't be a whore if you married me."

Archie took a step back from the powerful emotions brimming from every pore of his lover's body. He closed his eyes and reached deep inside himself for the mask he wore whilst in society.

"I'm sorry if you assumed I'd marry you, if you gave yourself to me."

Charlotte gasped and wrapped her arms around her body. Her eyes showed so much hurt and pain that Archie immediately wished the words back. Ruthlessly, he squashed the impulse to comfort her and instead started pulling on the rest of his soiled clothing, not caring that he could smell himself, and her, on his jacket.

Now that his brain wasn't fogged with the haze of passion, the voice of reason was reasserting itself. He had to keep her away from him. One more moment of intimacy and he would be down on bended knee begging for her hand in marriage and damn the scandal. But he could never do that to her, never.

"Charlotte, I know that one day you will find a man to marry who deserves you, but it's not me."

Charlotte just stared at him, then asked the one question he never thought she would ask.

"You don't love me?"

Archie jerked back as though she had struck him. Unable to lie to her face, he turned his back on her, so he faced the fireplace.

There was only one answer he could give. "No, I don't."

"Look at me when you break my heart, at least."

Archie closed his eyes in agony, yet turned at her request, hopeful his heart was now firmly locked away.

"I'm sorry if I have hurt you, Charlotte, but it is for your own good. Listen to me. Find someone to marry whose name isn't going to be scorned for the next century."

"So, you don't love me?" she repeated the question, apparently aware of the fact that he was avoiding lying to her face.

Archie steeled himself to lie again, but he wasn't sure if he had the strength. This was truly going to kill all and any feeling Charlotte had for him. He opened his mouth but was saved by a knock at the door.

"My lord, the solicitor is here to see you," his butler announced through the door.

"Thank you, Hill," Archie choked out, "Lady Charlotte requires her cloak, and I will need a few moments before attending to the solicitor. Put him in the morning room."

Archie heard the butler leave and sent a prayer of thanks for discreet and loyal servants.

"Go home, Charlotte. Thank you for your...condolences and support, but I think you must go."

Charlotte made an incoherent noise in her throat, and Archie turned away to open the door for the butler. He could barely breathe. Keeping a calm façade was taking every ounce of strength he had.

Archie was stunned by the pain he was in. Charlotte was acting like she was in love with him, and what had she said?

"At least look at me when you break my heart." Oh God, she couldn't love him, she just couldn't. That would be too cruel.

"Lady Charlotte's cloak, my lord." Hill opened the door, bowed and handed Archie Charlotte's cloak. He took one look at Archie's ruffled and soiled appearance and nodded once, his face inscrutable.

"If you will permit me, sir, I will walk Lady Charlotte out, and you can see your valet in your room, before the solicitor."

The quiet suggestion brought home to Archie just what he must look like. Clothes that had clearly been removed and then hastily re-donned and the scent of male completion lingering in the air. Sick disgust twisted his gut.

He nodded once to Hill and held open the door for his heart to leave him once and for all.

Tears spilled down Charlotte's reddened cheeks, and she didn't even bother to wipe them away. She simply took her cloak, wrapped it around herself and followed Hill from the room.

Chapter Thirteen

Archie had thought the pain of losing his brother and his place in society would be hard, and for ten years, he had done everything in his power to prepare for the worst. He had realised very soon after Charlotte left his study that nothing he had ever experienced before came close to how he felt now.

It had been a month since he had made love to his one and only love, and he felt like she had walked away with his soul when she had left his home. He had nothing left inside of him. His heart beat so slowly that it was painful feeling its rhythm inside his chest every waking minute.

In full mourning and also in full disgrace, Archie did not venture out of doors. He did not go for rides, he did not go to his club, and he did not see his friends. He had always thought that when the time came, he would be content with his estate business. Meeting with the land manager, his broker, his banker, and the attorney. He would read his books at night, and he would be content. How wrong could one man be?

He missed his old life so much it choked him. He woke in the middle of the night struggling to breathe, sweat running off him. He had taken to bathing twice a day just to pass the time.

He missed the time with his horses. He missed wasting time talking to Oliver or pretending to drink with Rupert.

Archie had always assumed that once he became his father's heir and the worst was known, he could turn into an ordinary gentleman. He could drink all night, tup whores and gamble away his money. Instead of feeling free and rebellious, he was sad and empty. He would give anything to have his stoic, boring life back. To be able to marry the one woman he loved and by all impossible accounts, probably loved him too.

That was the real rub. The look on Charlotte's face when he had told her he still wouldn't marry her, even after they had shared the most amazing experience of his life. It had almost slain him. He would have preferred a public lashing over watching her face crumble, and her heart break at his feet. She had been so courageous, so brave, and he had been a coward.

How could he have turned his back on her when she knew the worst about his family, and yet she still wanted to marry him; be with him? He had spent the last ten years convincing himself that no woman would ever forgive him for tying her to a family with his reputation, and yet she had willingly come to him *after* she had found out. She had given herself to a man worth nothing in the eyes of so much of the *ton*.

Could she not care? Could she be willing to marry him—even love him? Despite everything?

It had taken a whole month of wallowing in his stupidity and pouring all of his efforts into rebuilding his father's neglected estate for him to realise that his friends hadn't turned their backs on him either, as he had expected. He had turned his back on them.

It was unbelievable, really. He had spent ten years fearing the worst, and now he was doing his best to make it come true.

All three of the original "spares" had been by numerous times, together and separately, trying to visit him and he had turned them all away. At the time, he had told himself that he was protecting them, but wasn't he just protecting himself? From the hurt he assumed they were about to bestow by cutting him off? Or could he just not face their condolences and pity?

That was more likely, he acknowledged. He didn't want men who had once respected his opinion and his self-control, pitying him. Or worse, realising that he had been faking his perfection under a tremendous amount of fear for most of his adult life.

Archie saw his life mapped out ahead of him. Decades of lonely days and even more desolate nights. He would be totally alone until he could convince some down-on-her-luck spinster to marry him, to continue the line. Knowing he could never love her the way he loved Charlotte.

Archie stood up suddenly and had to sit down again just as quickly. When was the last time he had eaten? He had no idea.

All at once he knew what he had to do. He had to get a special licence to marry Charlotte as soon as possible. They had an uncle on his mother's side who was a bishop. He would grant Archie what he needed. They were still in full mourning so a marriage would be looked down upon, regardless of his current situation. However, Archie knew that he would need more than just words to convince Charlotte that he desperately wanted to marry her. After all he'd put her through, he'd be lucky if she would have him now.

Feeling a spark inside of him stir to life, a purpose that he hadn't felt in a very long time, he ran to his rooms to change. He would organise a special licence today and call upon her tomorrow. He had a purpose now, and nothing and no one was going to stand in his way.

CHARLOTTE HAD SPENT the last month wishing she were dead and the last two days wishing she were buried so that no one could ever find her. How could she have been so stupid? Not only had she given Archie the most prized possession of any gently bred lady, but she had also given him her heart, and now she was lost without it.

Her energy was running out. She couldn't continue to pretend that everything was fine. She had tried to keep her routine so no one would know something was wrong. She went shopping with her maid for more dresses, gloves, and shoes that she had no intention of wearing. Attended afternoon teas with her mother, listening to people gossip about who was marrying whom, and whether anyone had seen Archie. If she had to speak to one more insipid lady, she would scream.

To make matters worse, she had been vomiting throughout the day. The smell of any meat turned her stomach. She could hardly get out of bed in the morning and was starting to worry that it was something more than a broken heart causing these things.

Charlotte sat in the afternoon sitting room, embroidering, when she heard the welcome sound of her friend's voice.

"The Duchess of Lincoln," their butler announced.

Sarah breezed through the door looking beautiful, her sky-blue dress perfectly offsetting her golden hair and cornflower blue eyes. Charlotte hadn't seen Sarah in three months, as her husband had whisked her off to their country estate after her bed rest had been completed.

"Sarah." Charlotte lay her embroidery aside and stood up to curtsey. She greeted her friend with the biggest smile she had conjured up in over a month.

"Charlotte." Sarah greeted her with a kiss on both cheeks, her warmth a balm to Charlotte's frayed nerves.

"What's happened?" Sarah asked with a worried tone, then drew Charlotte over onto the chaise.

Hot tears welled up in Charlotte's eyes, and she opened her mouth to spill something of her pain. The door swung open again, and her brother and Sarah's husband joined them.

"Are you crying again?" John asked rudely, his face set in a grimace.

"John Dunford!" Sarah scolded, as Charlotte's eyes filled to the point of overflowing.

John groaned and pointed at Charlotte. "I'm sorry, Sarah. But something is seriously wrong with her, and she won't talk to anyone."

"John, please..." Charlotte begged. She had thought she hid her melancholy well from her family.

"Tea and custard, your favorite, Lady Charlotte." A maid came in bearing a huge tray of saucers and desserts.

The smell of warm milky custard wafted up to Charlotte's nose, and before she could contain it, vomit erupted up her throat. She ran to the corner and deposited the tiny amount of food in her stomach into a potted plant there.

John groaned. "This is what I mean. She has been moping around the house for weeks and now she's sick all the time."

Charlotte thanked Oliver for his offered handkerchief and wiped her mouth. Despite the fact that she should have excused herself and gone upstairs, she moved slowly back over to Sarah's side while the maid removed the pot plant.

Charlotte sat down with a weary sigh, picked up a cup of tea Sarah had poured and sipped slowly. The taste of stomach acid lingered in her mouth, and she was pleased when the maid returned to collect the custard and the tray from the room.

Sarah's eyes seemed to be cataloguing all of her symptoms and with a little gasp, she hissed into Charlotte's ear.

"Charlotte, you're not!"

Charlotte paled at the horrified look Sarah was giving her, her stomach wrenching painfully. She was going to lose all of her friends and family when everyone ealized what she had done.

"She's not, what?" John asked, his tone one of bewilderment.

"I thought it was just a stomach complaint, but putting it all together, it makes sense," Charlotte admitted to her friend, collapsing further into her seat.

She hadn't had her monthly flux, and she was so tired and sick all the time it could only mean one thing.

Instead of shying away from her as Charlotte had expected, Sarah moved closer and was holding Charlotte within her arms in seconds. Heat surrounded her, and Charlotte gave in and sobbed against her friend.

"What are you going to do?" Sarah whispered into Charlotte's ear, rocking her as though she were an infant.

"I believe I'll retire to our country estate this year and stay for a while," Charlotte said calmly, pushing herself up to a seated position again.

She finally accepted that her night with Archie had created consequences beyond what they had both imagined.

The light of comprehension was dawning in Oliver's eyes, but John was still at a loss regarding what was going on.

"The Earl of Totherham," their butler announced. This was Archie's new title.

Charlotte put her head on Sarah's shoulder and clung to her hand. This day could not get any worse. She had wanted Archie to come to her for over a month, and today was the day he chose?

Sarah gave her a suspicious look and held her harder. Charlotte let another tear escape and allowed her friend, who was once a vicar's daughter, to give her the comfort she so desperately needed.

ARCHIE'S HEART was thumping so loudly he was surprised he could hear the butler as he was announced over the roaring in his ears. He was shocked to find such a large group assembled in the parlour as he entered, but he bowed politely.

He moved toward Charlotte. He had spent an hour with his valet, preparing for this moment, and he didn't want to pretend indifference. He was shaved and oiled, pressed and perfectly dressed.

"Charlotte, may I have a private word?" he asked, skipping the formalities. His throat was raw and sore from too much drinking and the silent screaming of the past month.

Charlotte shook her head in answer, and a silvery tear slipped down her cheek. Archie's heart clenched hard in his chest. *Why was she crying?*

"Tell me what the hell is going on!" John fairly yelled, and Archie took a step back, shocked. What had he walked into?

"My apologies, John. I didn't realise I interrupted something."

John waved his hand dismissively.

"You didn't, Archie. All I know is that Charlotte has been ill for weeks and now she's talking about retiring to the country until next season. Why would you do that, Charlotte? You know we don't go out there." John addressed his sister with a stern tone of voice. He was apparently baffled, but there was a wealth of meaning in his words that Charlotte was obviously ignoring.

It hit Archie like a lead weight. He took in her face, the faint smell of vomit in the room and his actions of a month ago.

"You're pregnant," he breathed, unable to believe it and yet speaking the words as soon as they entered his mind.

"She's what?" John and Oliver both yelled.

"Impossible, tell them it's impossible," John urged Charlotte, taking a step closer to his weeping sister.

Charlotte closed her eyes and seemed to sway against Sarah, the two women locking together like limpets to rock.

Opening her eyes, she took a deep breath and Archie held his breath, waiting for the words that would determine his future.

"It's true."

Archie gasped, and John wheeled back and collapsed into a chair.

"Who, for God's sake?"

Archie opened his mouth to interrupt, but Charlotte was refusing to look at him. She sat up straighter, moving away from Sarah to address the room.

"The father has refused to marry me so I will be having the baby in the country and will stay there. I have no wish to burden my family with the stain that this will cause, but I will not give it up either."

Guilt hit Archie hard, with burning hot intensity. Did she believe such a thing?

"He won't marry you? What sort of bounder seduced you?" Oliver cried.

"Was it rape?" Sarah asked from next to Charlotte, the only one brave enough to ask the question.

Oh, God, no!

"No," Charlotte cried, sitting back down next to Sarah and squeezing her hands.

"Well, we'll find someone else to marry you. You are not giving birth to a bastard, Charlotte. Maybe someone who needs an heir but hasn't any children..." John was mumbling now, thinking about possibilities and options for his beloved sister.

Archie hadn't moved since Charlotte had announced that she was, indeed, with child. He felt as though he had been hit with a mallet, unmoving and pained. He had finally decided that enough was enough, he would beg Charlotte to forgive him and to marry him, and now she had to. He should have felt relieved, but he didn't. He wanted her to choose him because he loved her, not because there was a child.

He then heard the words John was raving, and his control snapped.

"Stop!" he roared, pushing his hands out to the room as though he could halt the insanity around him.

Archie staggered over to Charlotte and went down on his knees in front of her. He reached for her hands and clasped both of hers in his. She looked up at him with tear-stained eyes, and his heart did a little misstep.

"Marry me," he urged, squeezing her hands for emphasis.

"No." Charlotte shook her head and bit her lip, two more tears slipping down her pale cheeks.

"Yes," he insisted, holding onto her hands when she tried to pull them away.

Archie heard a growl behind him, knowing it was John and shivering at the prospect. He also knew he had only seconds left before a fist would land somewhere on his body.

"I love you. I have loved you since you were sixteen-years old and debuted in the most horrible white dress I have ever seen. Marry me, please."

Archie had so much more to say, but hands were pulling at him, and he had to let go of Charlotte's hands so that he could confront his friend.

John and Oliver pulled him to his feet and spun him around.

"Why are you offering to marry her, Archie?" John asked, his face a mixture of fear, anger, and trepidation.

"Because I love her, I have always loved her. I just didn't want to offer for her when my family's name was so badly ruined. But now, I have no choice. I must."

"You're proposing to marry her, despite the baby? Or because of the baby?" John asked, his face showing signs of hope and fear, warring.

Archie took a deep breath and told the truth, knowing full well what was going to happen, and he deserved it.

"Both…it's my baby," he announced quietly. The stillness in the room meant the words echoed as though he had shouted.

Chapter Fourteen

John's fist ploughed directly into his jaw, causing Archie to spin backwards, pain splintering across his face and through his brain.

John was on him in a second, pummeling his stomach until he was hauled away by Rupert and Oliver.

"You bastard," John hissed, breathing like he'd finished ten rounds in a boxing ring.

Archie fell into a chair, breathless, his lip bleeding and beginning to swell already. He coughed, his ribs screaming at him.

Charlotte pulled the cord for the butler and ran to him, throwing herself into his lap and covering his face in kisses and touches.

"Oh, my love, are you hurt? Show me, show me." She ran her hands, soothing but frantic, all over him.

Archie winced as his bruised body screamed out in pain but gathered her close despite it. He wanted to press his head to her breasts and let her comfort him, but he heard another low growl and knew he needed to have it out with John first.

"Darling, would you and Sarah go upstairs for a little while? I need to talk to your brother." Archie choked out the words as soothingly as he could, considering he had been punched in the stomach only a moment before, and his breath was still missing.

"But..." Charlotte half-protested, her gaze flicking between Archie and her angry brother.

"It will be all right," he reassured her, and despite their audience, he pressed a quick kiss to her lips.

"Charlotte, please." He stood up slowly and pushed her gently towards Sarah.

For the first time, Archie looked at Charlotte. She did look pale and extremely tired, and yet she'd never looked more beautiful to him. A child, *their* child. He could barely believe it.

"You'll be married next week," John declared from where he was forcibly held down.

Charlotte stamped her foot. "John, you cannot tell us what to do!"

Archie pulled out the piece of paper he had in his breast pocket.

"I organised a special licence yesterday," he told Charlotte, with eyes only for her.

"Even before you knew?" She trailed off, her hand sliding down to cover her belly, her womb, containing his child.

He followed the path of her hand and then looked back up to her face.

"Yes. I love you," he repeated, this time quietly, only for her benefit.

Charlotte's smile was brilliant, warming him from the inside out. She then left the room with Sarah. As he had requested.

One down, one to go.

"You better have a good explanation for this, Tother."

Archie flinched at John's use of his new title. It was not a good start to the conversation, but Archie reined in his wild emotions and sat in the chair opposite John. Rupert and Oliver had a firm grip on John's shoulders and Archie trusted them not to let their friend have his head, and pound Archie into the dust. Although technically he deserved it, he didn't want to get married looking like a bloody mess.

"The only explanation, John, is that I lost my mind."

John growled. "If I hear one insult about my sister, I am going to wring your neck."

"No, John, you misunderstand me," Archie quickly corrected, holding up his hands in a peaceful entreaty. "I love your sister, I always have. But there is no excuse for the fact that I made love to her before we were married. None."

John's shoulders sagged when Archie openly admitted he was wrong.

"Then why? For God's sake, Archie! Why?"

"I have known about my brother's illness since the week before I turned eighteen." Archie had decided it was best to explain everything.

They all went silent, looking at each other with surprised expressions, but it was Rupert who put it all together.

"So that's why you wouldn't come to the brothel, then or ever," Rupert said.

"Yes. My father informed me that I would be his heir and that I was to keep myself out of the whorehouses." Archie kept his chin high but had to break his composure to wipe the blood off his chin as it began to drip toward his clothes.

"So where does Charlotte come into this?" John growled again, his eyes narrowed, his jaw clenched.

Archie counted himself lucky that they were sitting in a reception room and not John's study where his dueling pistols were kept.

"I would have courted Charlotte and proposed years ago, but I was always terrified of what would happen when everyone found out how my brother died. I feared that even if I kept my reputation spotless, people would still paint me with the same brush," Archie confessed, feeling the load that he had carried on his shoulders for so long lift from him. It felt good to confess his fears and secrets. He had been so stupid to keep it to himself for so long.

"So? What happened?" Rupert asked. Releasing his hand from John's shoulder, he kept one eye on John and the other eye on Archie.

"A few months ago, Charlotte and I started to talk and get to know each other better. I had spent so many years keeping her at arm's length that I just couldn't do it anymore."

"I always did wonder why you two had such an intense dislike for each other," Oliver murmured.

"Self-preservation, I'm afraid. Well, at least on my behalf," Archie told them quietly with a wry smile.

He wasn't sure if Charlotte had wanted him for all the years he had desired her, but he would find out soon enough.

"So...?" John prompted, sitting forward in his chair and apparently wanting more specific information.

Archie took a breath and guarded himself for the next attack.

"So, almost five weeks ago Charlotte visited me at my house to express her condolences..."

"By herself?" John asked, his face incredulous.

Archie nodded, trying not to put any of the blame on Charlotte, but not wanting John to think he set out to seduce her either.

"And I was so totally out of my mind. I just couldn't fight her any longer."

"So, you ruined her," John said flatly, obviously still angry but looking quite defeated at the same time.

A wry smile touched Archie's lips.

"We ruined each other, I'm afraid. I could never have anyone else but her."

Archie looked around the room, and only Oliver smiled at that. He was the only one who knew what it felt like to make love, rather than the rutting variation in which his friends indulged.

"Then why did she say the father of her baby wouldn't marry her?" John asked now, that hard glitter reappearing in his eye.

Archie swallowed down his guilt and gave them the honest truth.

"Because, initially I told her I couldn't."

"You what?" John yelled, surging to his feet. Rupert and Oliver stayed close but didn't try to restrain him.

Archie dragged himself to his feet, not sure if he even had the strength to raise his arms if it came to a real fight. But John didn't seem interested in fighting, physically. He started pacing like a restless animal.

"You ruined her and then refused to marry her! What sort of gentleman are you?" John cried, obviously frustrated beyond bearing.

"John, I know I was wrong, so very wrong. But I preferred Charlotte to be able to marry someone with a good name. Someone who would be accepted by society, rather than be mine. How could I draw Charlotte into that scandal?" Archie knew that the argument had merit, but also knew that ruining her and not marrying her was an even greater offence.

John growled again, low in his throat.

"And yet, you did."

Archie only nodded. If he had known Charlotte was pregnant, he would have come to his senses weeks ago. That result had never even occurred to him, which showed how off his game he was.

"My father is expected home in an hour. You can have your meeting with him to discuss the settlement, and then you can be married."

Archie just nodded, his arms and legs feeling weaker by the second.

"Archie, are you all right?" John asked, concerned now.

His head was spinning. The blackness came in to claim him and after weeks of not eating or sleeping, he gave into it.

HE CAME BACK to consciousness with his head in Charlotte's lap and her refusing to let him go.

"If what you say is true and we will be married, possibly even tomorrow, then I have every right to hold him until he awakens. He's unconscious, for heaven's sake!" She sat on the floor with him, stroking his hair soothingly. Archie was loathe to open his eyes in case she stopped.

Charlotte must have felt his breathing change because she was soon asking, "Archie, are you awake? Open your eyes, my love."

He reluctantly blinked open his eyes and found himself still in the sitting room. He was surrounded by Charlotte, John, Oliver, Sarah, Rupert and four or five servants.

"I'm all right," he said, attempting to sit up. His head spun so fast that he lay back down again with a moan.

Charlotte wrapped her arms around him protectively and held him tight. The heat of her made him instantly relax, his eyes closing on a sigh.

"Archie, rest, please."

Someone growled at this.

Archie summoned the energy to open his eyes again. He asked, "May my fiancée and I have a few moments alone, please?"

He knew he must look ridiculous lying on the Aubusson rug with his head in Charlotte's lap, but he stayed where he was, nonetheless.

"I think you've had enough moments alone, don't you?" John asked, his tone dripping with sarcasm.

"John!" This admonition came from Sarah, and it was Oliver who finally stepped in to help them.

"I think they can have a moment alone to discuss their wedding."

He gathered the assembly like the duke he now was and swept out of the room.

"Are you sure you are fine?" Charlotte asked, her voice trembling.

Archie sat up slowly, swallowing the bile that rose in his throat and turned around to face her, his palms sweating.

"Me? How are you?" he asked, sliding his hand to her still flat stomach, feeling the softness there.

A strange happiness settled over him, something that had been missing from his life for a very long time.

Charlotte blushed crimson at his touch but did not move away. Instead, she moved into his touch, warming his heart all the more.

Chapter Fifteen

Charlotte had never known real terror until she had heard John calling for help because Archie was ill. She had spent half an hour pacing her room, answering all of Sarah's questions and reassuring her friend that it wasn't her fault. The poor woman had got it into her mind that it was what she had advised that day in her sitting room that had led Charlotte to sleep with Archie.

Charlotte was happily relating how wonderful it had been when she had heard the yell. Not mindful of anything but getting to Archie as quickly as she could, she flew down the stairs and had dropped to her knees before him. Seeing him lying there, so still and pale, had made her feel like her insides had been scooped out. She'd thought he had broken her heart irretrievably, but she had been wrong. It seemed that the silly thing still beat only for him.

"I'm a little apprehensive about the immediate future, but otherwise, I feel fine," she told him honestly.

"You'll be all right. *We'll* be all right, Charlotte. You and the baby are going to be healthy and well. We'll travel to my father's estate for our honeymoon, and just decide not to come back until next season."

Charlotte's smile faltered. She wasn't worried about the scandal or the baby. She was worried that Archie was only marrying her because she had trapped him. It was the oldest trick in the book on how to land a good husband, and she hated herself for it. She was sure he despised her for it, too.

Charlotte dropped her head and refused to look at him.

"What's wrong?" Archie asked, pulling them both up and onto the chaise lounge, placing her on his lap and wrapping his arms around her.

"Everything," she cried, letting her tears fall.

Archie crooned and stroked her hair, telling her that everything was going to be all right.

John chose that moment to stick his head in and just as quickly stuck it back out again.

"Charlotte, I'm sorry you're going to have to marry me. If I could have saved you from this pain, I would have."

Charlotte laughed, the sound somewhere between a sob and a gulp. Pulling her head up so that she could look at him, she put all her strength into her glare. "I want to marry you. I've always wanted to marry you."

Archie pulled out his handkerchief and blotted her face, the move so endearing as to make her sob again. He truly was a gentleman.

"Then why are you crying?" he asked gently.

"Because you don't want to marry me." She whispered the feared words, biting her lip as the tears began to fall down her face again in unending hot waves.

Archie cradled her face in both of his hands and forced her gaze up to his.

"Charlotte, listen to me and listen carefully. The only, and I mean the only, reason I have not asked you to marry me before now, was that I couldn't bear the idea of you being cut directly or embarrassed by my family's reputation being ruined. I couldn't bring you into that."

"So that stopped you from asking me? For how long?" she whispered, fear and hope flaring alive in her heart.

His eyes told her that he was speaking the truth, and it would be in Archie's character to protect her in such a way.

"Years. Almost since the moment I met you again at your coming out. I fell in love with your wit and your fire, your passion for life and your wicked sense of humour. You are also the most beautiful woman I have ever seen in my life."

Charlotte blushed at his words and wrapped her arms around his neck.

"So, you do love me," she whispered again, tendrils of hope heating a path of light through her heart and body.

"I do," he repeated and pressed his soft lips to hers.

It had been forever since they had kissed, or that was how it felt to Charlotte. Her lips clung to his, and she moaned loudly when he encouraged her lips to open. He swept his tongue into her mouth.

A loud noise, a throat being cleared, brought them both back to reality.

A smiling Oliver and a red-faced John stood in the doorway.

Charlotte blushed again and stood up. Archie followed more slowly. Oliver turned away with a smile, and John started turning purple.

"I think it's time for you to wait in the library," John told Archie with a look that brooked no argument.

Archie turned to Charlotte and bowed over her outstretched hand.

"Get some rest, my dear." He gave her a wink that was at odds with his formal words and left the room.

Charlotte straightened from her curtsey to see John staring at her.

His analytical gaze roamed over her face and he sighed loudly.

"You're looking better already."

IT TOOK VERY little time to work out Charlotte's wedding settlement. Once her father had been informed about Charlotte's condition, it was pretty much settled. He called Archie a few choice names, which Archie agreed with, and then they went on to discuss the financials.

Archie was pleased to realise he could easily afford the pin money her father was currently giving her, and he even signed a document to make sure she kept the property she owned in her name. He had no wish to take anything away from her. From what she had originally said about her not wanting to marry because of her future husband's power over her, he was determined to give her as much freedom as possible.

Her dowry was also very generous. It had been increased from ten to fifteen thousand pounds as she had remained unmarried, and although Archie would have liked to refuse it outright, he was soon told that it was not negotiable. He found it amusing that they thought he might back out of the wedding if he didn't get everything to which he was entitled. Maybe Charlotte would like to invest it for the baby, or go for a European trip? He'd ask her in a few days' time.

Later that evening, Archie found himself inside the library of Rupert's bachelor townhouse. He was still contemplating the wisdom of his visit when the devil himself walked in.

"Archie, my man. Come to enjoy your last night as a single man?" His friend asked the question jovially, a bottle of port in his left hand and a bottle of brandy in his right.

"I've come for some advice, Rupert," Archie told his friend. He tried not to sound as horrified as he actually was, to be asking such things.

"Will you have a drink?" Rupert asked, the resigned look in his eye telling Archie that he didn't expect a "yes."

Archie hardly ever drank spirits. He had always avoided anything that eroded his self-control.

"Yes," he said with a definite nod. "Port, fill it up."

He was going to need courage tonight, and if that courage came in a bottle, then so be it.

Rupert's eyebrows shot up, but he didn't say anything, just filled up a glass of expensive port and gestured to a chair.

Archie reached for his drink and swallowed half of the glass in one gulp, almost choked, and then sat down slowly in the chair.

Again, Rupert's eyebrows shot up, but he didn't say anything about Archie's uncharacteristic display.

"So, I should congratulate you on your upcoming marriage. Charlotte's probably the only sane woman in the *ton*. And a duke's daughter, too. You've done well."

Archie smiled at Rupert's attempt at light conversation. The man was as subtle as a cow in a sitting room.

"Yes, I have. Despite everything." Archie still couldn't believe he was marrying one of the few ladies of the *ton* who any man would give his eye teeth to have.

"Archie, you know that none of us think any less of you because your brother was...unlucky." Rupert looked down at his port, and Archie felt the usual anger swelling in his gut.

"Unlucky," Archie repeated, finding the word grossly inadequate.

"I'm sorry, Archie, I don't know what else to say," Rupert said gruffly, obviously uncomfortable with the topic. He gave a shrug and Archie felt a little sorry for his whore-mongering friend.

"Look, Rupert, my brother's death was horrible and gruesome. If the details help put you off bedding every whore in London, then I will be happy to share."

Rupert opened his mouth, but Archie held up his hand.

"I came here for advice about bedding, so I shouldn't disparage you for having the experience I need. Forgive me."

Rupert nodded stiffly, but the burning anger in his eyes remained.

"What do you want to know?" he asked through slightly clenched teeth.

"I want to know what else I can do, other than what I already know," Archie said quickly, swallowing the rest of his port and gesturing for more.

"Tell me what you know and we'll go from there." Rupert smiled, and Archie knew his friend thought this a great joke. To have the prude come to the rake for advice was quite the back flip for Archie.

"Charlotte—" He stopped. How could he share what he and Charlotte had experienced?

Rupert cleared his throat loudly.

"I think it might be better if we just talk about bedding and women in general. I don't think I can stand thinking about Charlotte that way."

Archie looked at Rupert, a little puzzled about the slight flush staining his friend's handsome face. Then he remembered that Oliver and Rupert thought of Charlotte very much like a younger sister, a feeling he had never shared.

"Well, I touched and kissed her breasts."

"Ah... the woman's breasts, please." Rupert brought up his hands to cover his ears in an age-old gesture of not wanting to hear what was being said.

"Sorry, the woman I bedded a month ago. I touched and kissed her breasts." Archie grinned at his friend. It was vastly amusing that Rupert should be so flustered.

"Sucked too?" Rupert asked.

"Yes, but not much," Archie said with a slight frown. He wasn't quite sure if he had done that correctly.

"Most women enjoy sucking, harder than you think they want, but less than you want to."

"All right. Then I touched her between her legs until she came and then I climbed on top." Archie flushed at the memory and buried his face in his glass once again.

"She came just from touching?" Rupert asked, skeptically.

"And licking," Archie admitted, blushing completely for the first time since he'd arrived.

Rupert cleared his throat again, obviously as uncomfortable with this conversation as Archie. "And you know that she *came*?"

"Yes," Archie nodded. He tried to pretend he was answering questions about something less personal, like the weather.

"How?" Rupert asked.

Archie clenched his teeth. He had asked for Rupert's advice, and now he had to be as honest as possible.

"Well, she cried out, shuddered and inside she...ah, clenched. Over and over again."

Now he was blushing again, the heat in his face rather uncomfortable. Inside his trousers, his prick would usually be swelling at the memory of his time with Charlotte, but one look at Rupert's face and his prick stayed calm.

"You have my felicitations, my friend. Most men don't care anything about a woman's pleasure. They don't even realise it is possible for a woman to orgasm."

"I have listened to you, drunk, over the years and picked up on a few things you know," Archie told Rupert honestly, giving credit where credit was due.

One of the only reasons he knew anything about what to touch or to expect with Charlotte, was due to the boasting Rupert did whilst in his cups.

Rupert choked on his port and then started to laugh, really laugh, like they had back in school.

Archie smiled at the sound, wondering why he couldn't remember the last time he'd heard such a deep happiness in his friend's voice.

"So, what sort of advice do you need? It sounds like you could give lessons, Archie."

"I want to know the best way of positioning her. Can you do it other ways than just on top?" Archie was shocked at his forthrightness, but as he watched Rupert fill up his glass for at least the third time, he knew why. "And any other pointers?"

God, he was slurring now.

"Well, there's three main ways and a hundred versions within them. You on top, her on top, or from behind." Rupert was starting to get into this instructor role now, his eyes glittering excitedly.

"Her on top? Are you jesting?" Archie just couldn't imagine it. How would that work? How could he move if she was sitting on top?

Rupert chuckled, then smothered it with a cough.

"It's true. Not many ladies of the *ton* would try it as they don't even like going to bed with their husbands. But that's the three."

"From behind?" Archie asked skeptically now. How? As horses mated? That was a rather unsettling thought.

"Yes, most women I know love that one. You can lie down, kneel or stand, and you can position her legs any way you want."

Archie's body stirred as he imagined the possibilities. If she was on her knees leaning forward, yes, he could see how that could work. Then another consideration surged to the front of his alcohol-hazed brain.

"But what if your bed partner is...ah...pregnant?"

Rupert looked shocked at the question but then the penny dropped, and he looked uncomfortable again.

"Honestly, I've never bedded a pregnant woman, Archie. You might want to ask Oliver." He was avoiding Archie's eyes now.

"Can you guess, though?" Archie asked.

This was imperative. He knew that his mother had taken to her bed as soon as she was pregnant with both his brother and himself, never to stir until after the birth. Was it safe for pregnant women to be as active as he hoped to be with his new wife?

"Well, I can imagine it comes down to comfort for you both. Although as she gets bigger, I would suggest on your knees from behind." Rupert was again avoiding looking directly at Archie. Archie had to assume it was due to the questions being more personal, as Rupert didn't want to think of Charlotte in that way.

"No...other tips?" Archie asked, barely able to get the words out as his tongue grew fuzzier and the heat from his belly spread down his arms and into his legs.

"Just enjoy the experience, my friend; you've waited long enough."

Archie grinned and knocked back the rest of his port. That was exactly what he intended to do.

Chapter Sixteen

The wedding was a small and private affair. There hadn't been time for Charlotte to have a custom-made wedding dress, so she'd had a team of seamstresses brought in, who had worked through the night to alter her mother's dress to fit her. It looked beautiful. A high neck with white lace embroidery, a tight-fitting bodice, and flowing white chiffon for the skirt.

Due to Archie's family still being in full mourning, the wedding had to be small, and most of the guests were wearing black or another sombre colour. Charlotte didn't see any of that. All she saw as she walked down the aisle on her father's arm was the man she loved. And by his admission, Archie loved her too.

The ceremony was short, but no one in the church doubted the way the bridegroom and bride felt about each other. Charlotte and Archie glowed with love for each other, their eyes telling the world just how happy they were.

Later that same day, they journeyed to Archie's family estate twelve miles from London. During the ride Charlotte's stomach churned, and they had to stop every hour for her to be sick or get some fresh air. Archie tried to make her stop at an inn in a nearby town, but she was determined to be in their marital bed that night. She had missed Archie with every beat of her heart, and although the pregnancy had made her very strange in the stomach, it had also made other parts of her body newly sensitive.

Charlotte had lain awake in her bed the night before her wedding, taking an inventory of her new body. Her breasts were slightly larger, and her nipples were even more sensitive. She had shyly run her hand down between her legs just to see if that too had changed and had been shocked at the level of feeling even her own hand could elicit. She couldn't wait to be taken to bed, a proper bed this time, and make love to her husband.

"We're here, Charlotte." Archie's voice floated through her dream, and she came awake slowly.

Charlotte's eyes fluttered open. "Archie, it's lovely." She sighed as she took in the well-cared for gardens and a new extension.

Archie helped her down from the carriage, her legs wobbling slightly when they touched the ground. Archie dove to catch her and there, in front of almost every servant of the estate, her new husband kissed her. Lovingly, slowly and thoroughly.

Charlotte was enjoying the feel of Archie's warm, thick lips on hers when he seemed to stiffen and lift away from her. Frowning at the loss of contact, she raised her hands up to his hair to pull him back down, when she noticed fifty pairs of eyes looking at them. Or trying not to look at them, was perhaps a better description. Blushing furiously, she allowed Archie to pull her up and to his side.

Clearing his throat, he introduced her to the principal staff members and then she was shown straight to her room to freshen up.

Charlotte put on her most daring evening gown, cut in a French design that barely covered her breasts. She had never actually worn it, buying it in a rebellious mood and then never having the courage to wear it in company. However, as a newly-married woman, she had packed it knowing it would come in handy, especially if she wanted Archie to carry her off to bed as soon as it was feasible.

She was shown into the dining room by the butler. The footman who opened the door could barely keep his eyes away from her bosom.

Archie approached her with a look of calm on his face but it seemed schooled rather than genuine.

"My dear, you look lovely."

Charlotte was instantly disappointed. Was that all she got? Her nipples were about to pop out in front of ten footmen, and Archie thought she looked "lovely?"

Pasting a fake smile on her face, she sat down to their dinner.

They chatted amiably about their day and the house, over five courses.

During dessert, Archie couldn't seem to keep his eyes on her face any longer, and kept dropping to her cleavage. "Is that a new dress, Charlotte?" he asked casually.

"Not at all, my lord, I've had it for three years."

She swallowed a sip of her wine and watched for the tiny signs of distress upon his face. If she hadn't known Archie well, she wouldn't have seen the slight downward tilt of his mouth and the stillness of his body.

She stilled too, and waited for the next question.

Archie spooned a piece of apple pie into his mouth. Then he asked with a smooth and gentle tone, "You've worn it often, then?"

Charlotte feigned shock and ignored the question.

"You don't like it, my lord? I am so sorry. I had forgotten how much you enjoy fashion. Should I change into something more suitable for the rest of the evening?"

With a completely straight face Archie told her, "Oh, yes, my dear, it pays to stay in fashion. I believe that we shall have to stay here at the estate. We can't have you wearing such an outdated dress in company."

Charlotte was so disappointed she could barely prevent tears from rolling down her cheeks. She truly couldn't tell if he was teasing her or not. Maybe he was disgusted with the weight she'd put on? Maybe he didn't like her showing off flesh that should be kept on the inside of her dress?

She wiped away a single tear that escaped down her cheek. Then Archie pushed back his chair with a squeal as the chair leg scraped the floor.

He rushed straight over to her and bowed.

"Charlotte, would you join me for a drink in the music room?"

Charlotte nodded and stood up, her dessert all but forgotten. Her stomach churned and her eyes filled with more salty tears.

Walking her into the music room, Archie shut the door behind them and with a small twist he pushed her up against the wall.

"Archie," she cried, shocked but thrilled as her husband finally showed signs of wanting her.

He swooped down for a hot, passionate, and wet kiss. He demanded and she gave. He pressed his erection into her, and she moaned as she ran her hands through his hair.

Thank God, he's not angry!

Archie pulled back to look at her and smiled down at her. She knew her face was flushed, but she was too excited about her husband's hands on her to worry about how she looked.

"I can't stand the idea of anyone else seeing you in this dress, Charlotte. I'm sorry that you thought I was serious. I was just feeling very jealous that other people had seen these amazing breasts and I was trying to make a joke to defuse my jealousy. I'm not sure that it worked."

Whilst he spoke, Archie reached up and scooped her breasts out of the tiny piece of silk that held them in.

Charlotte gasped and then moaned as he softly pinched each nipple with his fingers, while he simultaneously bit down on the side of her neck.

His possessiveness was affecting her differently than she thought it would. Charlotte had always thought a jealous and possessive husband would be a hindrance, but she was finding it so exciting her heart was tripping over itself. Her body was ready for him this very minute.

"No one has ever seen me in this dress, Archie," she whispered, arching her back so that he would repeat his caresses.

"But you said..." he began, lifting his head and giving her a confused look.

"I said the dress was three years old, which it is. But I never wanted to wear it before tonight. I wanted you to want me," she whispered.

"Oh, I want you, Charlotte." Archie groaned, licking across her collarbones.

"You haven't touched me all day," she sulked, pouting. But she was unable to stop herself from running her hands up his chest and clinging to his muscled shoulders.

"Not because I didn't want to. I was just so scared, with the pregnancy and the stress...I wasn't sure if you'd want me to ravish you in the daylight or wait 'til we could be in your bed, in the dark."

Charlotte laughed, so relieved she couldn't describe the sensation. They still had so much to learn about each other, but this was a good start.

"You mean, like our first time? So proper. On the floor, in the middle of the day? In your library?"

Archie blushed at this reminder.

"Shall we go to bed now, my wife?" Archie asked politely, stepping back and offering her his arm.

Charlotte pulled her dress back up over her breasts and nodded.

Without another word, Archie towed her along the hallway, past three footmen who all looked at the ground, up the carpeted staircase, and into the main bedroom. His bedroom.

"This is where you will sleep for the next seven months, and this is where you will give birth to our child," Archie whispered into Charlotte's ear as he applied himself to unlacing her gown.

Charlotte couldn't believe the overwhelming emotions threatening to engulf her. Archie had married her, he loved her, and now he was going to consummate their marriage in the ducal bedchamber. Charlotte wasn't sure if Archie had deliberately brought her to his room rather than hers, or if it had been unconscious. Either way, she was secretly thrilled. Did he want to sleep with her every night just like Sarah and Oliver did? A tear slid unheeded down her cheek.

Archie turned her around to kiss her and saw the tear.

"Or we can sleep in your room, if you prefer," he offered hastily.

Charlotte smiled up at her new husband and put every bit of happiness she was feeling into it. She noticed he hadn't offered to sleep separately.

"Archie, I'll sleep anywhere you are, my love. Anywhere."

A small smile crept onto Archie's face.

"The stables?" he asked, grinning so that it was obvious this time he was joking.

Charlotte pushed her tiny chemise off her shoulders and let it slither to the floor, leaving her naked.

"Anywhere," she repeated with quiet conviction as Archie looked his fill.

Charlotte was beginning to think she should have kept herself covered up, her husband took so long to react. Then Archie dropped to his knees in front of her. Looking up at her, he whispered, "You are so beautiful you make my heart ache."

He bent forward and kissed her belly with a reverence usually reserved for something holy. Resisting the urge to cry again, Charlotte brought her hands up and threaded her fingers through his thick, brown hair.

Rising from his kneeling position, he lifted Charlotte up and into his arms. She giggled and smiled at him as she clung to his shoulders. She loved how strong he was. Slowly, he lay her down in the large bed, the soft mattress cushioning her weight. The blankets had been turned down, and the room was warm from the fire that had been going all day.

Charlotte watched from the bed with hungry eyes as Archie stripped off his clothes.

To her, Archie was the perfect man. Taut and lean with a face so handsome it could have belonged to an angel.

He stripped off the last of his clothes and went to join her on the bed.

"No," Charlotte cried, sitting up to reach for him.

Archie paused, his eyebrows rising and his mouth tightening around the edges.

"I want to look at you. I didn't get to last time." She rushed to reassure him, her eyes greedily taking in every inch of her perfect man. The whipcord, strong muscles, his flat stomach, the large and thick appendage already thrusting forth from its bed of dark brown curls.

"Do I pass, ma'am?" Archie asked with a mock bow and a smile.

Charlotte couldn't help the answering tug deep between her legs as he smiled at her. *Pass?* He was not only utterly beautiful, but the fact that no other woman besides herself had ever seen this sight, gave her satisfaction deep inside her heart.

"I love knowing that no one else has ever seen you like this," she whispered, tearing up again.

Bloody pregnant nerves.

Archie's face sobered.

"And you will be the only one ever to see me like this, Charlotte. I promise," he vowed, moving over to lie down next to her on the bed.

Charlotte blinked rapidly, trying not to cry again. Archie knew her so well now. His gift of faithfulness was the only one she wanted.

"You'll never leave me now," Archie growled at her as he rolled over her, moaning at the contact as he lay down on top of her.

The feel of his bare flesh upon hers was startling, and they simultaneously moaned. His naked body came into full contact with hers, and his erection thrust impatiently between her legs. Charlotte instinctively opened her thighs and wrapped her legs around his narrow hips.

Chapter Seventeen

Archie gasped as his aching cock pressed into her wet entrance, naturally, easily, due to her position. He hadn't meant for that to happen so quickly. He had wanted to savour their connection, to build her up slowly to that amazing crescendo of pleasure. He reared back on his arms and tried to pull back. Charlotte moaned.

"No, Archie, come to me." She locked her legs in place and pulled him deeper into her willing body.

Archie was lost in her welcoming heat. How was she so ready for him from one kiss? He hadn't even licked her breasts or done any of the things he had been planning, and yet she was open and wet for him. He sank deeper, her muscles tugging him in further until he was sunk to the balls in her tight heat.

Charlotte moaned and pulled Archie's head down for a kiss.

He began moving, slowly at first and then with harder and longer strokes. Charlotte began thrashing against the bed, her hard nipples brushing the hairs of his chest in a way that was driving them both mad.

Archie made a split-second decision, needing this to be more than a quick tumble for both of them. He held on to her tightly and rolled them so that she lay on top of him. Moving her legs out from under him he kissed her and filled both his palms with her breasts.

When Rupert had suggested this position, Archie hadn't been quite sure how it would work. But now he knew why it would become one of his favourites. He had so much better access to her body from this position. He kneaded her left breast with his right hand and moved his other hand down to that spot between her legs where she loved to be touched.

Charlotte sat up straight and looked down at him. Lifting herself up by her thighs, she rose off him slightly and then moved down again, experimentally. Archie moaned at his wife's natural wantonness, and she smiled with triumph. She rose up again a little higher and came down hard.

Archie moaned louder this time, pleasure splintering through his body. Both his hands gripped her fleshy hips, urging her to move faster. He began lifting her on him and then bringing her down.

Charlotte grabbed both of his hands to stop him from controlling their movements and put them both on her breasts. He took a deep breath and let her take the lead. She began moving on him, up and down in a beautiful rhythm that pushed Archie closer and closer to the edge. He was surprised when she slowed down and began frowning.

"Archie, I need you to help please, I need…"

Archie felt himself careening toward a climax but knew she was not. He carefully lifted her off him and pushed her back down onto her back. Ignoring the need in his loins, he moved down her body so that he could suckle at her breasts. They were a darker red now, no longer pale pink. What had Rupert said? He should suck harder than he assumed she would want, but not as hard as he would want to.

Smiling to himself, Archie dipped his head and pulled one long nipple into his mouth and sucked. Softly at first, waiting for a response. Charlotte moaned and pulled his head harder into her. Archie complied, sucking harder until she gasped. Pulling back, he looked up and smiled.

"Too hard?" he asked.

Charlotte shook her head. "No, keep doing that please."

Archie grinned at her and attacked the other breast, enjoying the plump flesh and the sweet taste of her skin. He moved his hand down between her thighs and rubbed the little nub, the spot she so loved to be touched.

"Archie, please, I need you," Charlotte begged, tugging on Archie's head to try bringing him up to her.

Archie ignored her and kept up his dual assault. Tugging at her nipples with both his lips and his teeth, he suckled until she was pushing him closer again. He flicked that sweet bit of flesh until he heard it.

Charlotte cried out, clenched her legs together, trapping his hand whilst her body spasmed and shook. He loved watching her find bliss in his arms. There was nothing better.

When she stopped shuddering and opened her eyes, she held her arms out to him. Instead of immediately going to her as his cock begged him to do, he reared back onto his haunches and smiled.

"Could we try one more thing?" he asked, both nervous and excited to be asking for such a thing.

"Of course."

"Can you roll over onto your hands and knees?" he asked, making flipping signs with his hands.

Archie could tell he had shocked her, as Charlotte's eyes widened, but she did what he asked. She turned slowly; her face still flushed.

She rolled over onto her hands and knees, tucking her bottom under.

Archie enjoyed the sight of her beautiful, plump behind for one moment before laying a hand on her. She jumped as though stung, then relaxed as he stroked up her back and down.

Archie was a little worried. How was this going to work? Better if he could see what to do, he supposed.

"Open your legs for me," he murmured, surprised at how deep his voice had gone.

Charlotte gasped and arched her back a little as though she'd get up, but settled and opened her legs an inch. Archie chuckled softly and moved his hands down to her thighs, gently pushing them further apart.

He could tell she was trying to hide her flesh from his view and spoke soothingly to her, trying to ease her fears.

"Charlotte, you are the most beautiful thing I have ever seen. Show me how much you want me, show me where you need me." He stroked between her legs and she gasped again, moving unconsciously toward his hands.

She tilted her pelvis back for him and lowered her breasts to the bed. Archie groaned as her plump pink flesh came into view and his gut clenched with need. Now he understood. Charlotte was aroused and pink, wet and waiting for him. He knelt behind her, felt for her entrance with one hand and guided the thick head of his cock there. Pressing in once again, he was surrounded by newly tightened tissues and gasped at the pleasure.

His head swam, and he had to grip her hips to stop himself from falling away from her. She moaned softly, and he thrust in fully, sheathing himself to the hilt. Oh God, he had never been in her so deep. She was glorious.

Archie was too far gone to wait for her again, he thrust one last time and let go of his control. The hot wave consumed him, flowing down from his chest, spreading into his belly and settling into his balls as his cock pulsed, his seed spreading inside her.

Exhausted, and with his head spinning in the clouds, Archie waited a moment, gently stroking Charlotte's back. When his thighs began to shake, he pulled out of her body and they rolled together onto the bed.

Charlotte settled naturally against him, and Archie closed his eyes, smiling as they fell together into sleep.

~

When Charlotte woke, the sun was streaming in through the open curtains and Archie was stroking her back in gentle, repetitive motions. She came to herself slowly, the warmth of Archie's chest beneath her cheek and the salty smell of his skin in her nostrils.

The scent of their lovemaking lingered in the air and on the sheets. Charlotte blushed lightly at the memory of all they'd done on their wedding night. How could she have known that such pleasure could be found within her body?

"Good morning, wife," Archie greeted her, chuckling as he spoke.

"Good morning, husband," she answered, kissing his chest and then lifting herself up to look at him.

The dark circles under his eyes had faded, and he looked so heartbreakingly beautiful that her own heart skipped a beat.

"How are you feeling?" he asked, frowning as his eyes searched her face.

Charlotte closed her eyes as nausea crept in.

"Nauseous, and sore," she murmured, feeling tender in spots she hadn't felt since the first time they had made love. She lay back against the pillows, trying valiantly not to be sick.

Archie leaned away from her and brought back a dry piece of toast.

"The kitchen brought this up not so long ago. The housekeeper assured me it would settle your stomach."

Charlotte stared at Archie for a moment and then at the toast. Had he asked his housekeeper about her pregnancy already? When? Hot tingles in her eyes told her that tears threatened her composure as the full impact of his thoughtful gesture hit her.

"Don't cry, Charlotte. I'm sorry. Are you that sore? Do you want me to order a bath, or…"

Charlotte laughed through her tears and launched herself at her husband, kissing him soundly on the lips before snatching the toast from him. Laying back against the pillows again she took a tentative bite and waited for her body's reaction. Her stomach gurgled a little, but nausea stayed the same, no worse. She ate the whole piece slowly, and the sick feeling subsided.

"May I have my tea?"

Her considerate husband choked out a laugh and handed her a sweetened cup that she sipped gratefully. Incredible. She'd been so afraid to tell anyone about her condition that no one had helped her through it.

"Are you sure you're fine?" he asked again.

"I feel much better, thank you," she answered, sighing happily as her whole body relaxed.

"And your…uhh…" Archie made a vague motion to the lower half of her body and arched an eyebrow.

Charlotte hid a smile in her teacup.

"My…" she repeated, looking at him with an expression conveying as much innocence as possible.

Archie cleared his throat. "You said you were sore."

Charlotte laughed again.

"So, you can touch it and kiss it, but you can't say the word?"

Archie's mouth kicked up in amusement.

"I apologise, madam wife. How is your honey pot this morning?"

Charlotte choked on her tea and sprayed half of it across the bed.

Archie laughed out loud.

Charlotte shot him a murderous glare and dabbed at the wet spots on the quilt.

"My *honey pot* felt sore and bruised this morning, thanks to my lusty husband," Charlotte retorted.

"I could kiss it better…" Archie offered, trailing his hand under the sheet.

Charlotte flinched back, and his happy face sobered. "I'm sorry."

"No, don't apologise. I just need to have a long soak in the tub." Well, she hoped that's all she needed.

"And how's our baby this morning?" Archie asked quietly, running his palm gently over her lower belly.

Charlotte felt a shiver run through her whole body at his touch.

"Fine, I think," she answered just as quietly. She really should see a doctor and find out what the recommendations were for her condition.

"I hope it was all right to do everything we did last night."

Charlotte watched Archie's face and could see many different emotions flickering across his eyes. It was going to take years to learn how to read him properly, and she didn't feel like waiting that long.

"What are you thinking?"

Archie's face instantly cleared into a polite mask.

"No," Charlotte wailed. She pushed him onto his back and swung up over him.

"Charlotte, we can't..."

"Archie, I can't tell what you're thinking most of the time, so I need you to tell me. Tell me if you're worried about something. Tell me if you need something. The only way our marriage is going to survive is if we talk to each other."

Charlotte had her hands on his chest and her eyes bore into his. She was determined they would have a good marriage. If that meant physically restraining him on occasion, then she would.

Archie lifted his hands to caress her soft nipples, smoothing the sides of her flesh.

Charlotte noticed where his eyes were lingering and felt his arousal jutting up against her buttocks. Making a noise of frustration, she pulled the covers up around her upper body and glared at him.

"Tell me what was worrying you a moment ago."

"I can't remember," Archie murmured, pulling at the quilt she had firmly wrapped around her body.

"You said, you hoped we didn't hurt the baby," Charlotte reminded him, keeping a tight hold on her covers.

Archie opened his mouth, then closed it again.

"Oh, that. Yes, well, I thought that maybe I should have left you to sleep. Perhaps I should have gone to another room last night, so I wouldn't be tempted to make love to you again."

Charlotte smiled as she remembered the way Archie had woken her during the night and made love to her, slowly and very thoroughly. She moved down so that she could lay down on his chest but could still look at him. It took some maneuvering around his erection, but she managed it.

"Never apologise for making love to me. I loved every second of it."

"But, you're sore..."

"Of course, I am, it was only my second and third time. I'm sure it will get easier from now on."

Archie's smile showed a hint of relief. "So, the baby's fine?"

"The baby's fine," Charlotte confirmed, laying her head down onto Archie's chest again.

She let herself drift slowly back to sleep.

Chapter Eighteen

Archie left Charlotte sleeping peacefully and went to his study. He tried to attend to his ledgers and books, but they would not capture his attention. His beautiful wife had done far too good a job of that this morning.

Why would she want to know his thoughts and desires? Would she strive to give them to him, or would she use them against him?

He physically shook his head to dispel the thought. Charlotte would not use his desires against him.

Last night, she had not only allowed him every intimacy as her new husband, but she had been willing to try anything that he asked of her, seeming to enjoy everything as much as he had. And, God had he enjoyed it. He wasn't sure how long he could wait to bed her again.

No, she needed rest. He didn't want her shying away from him because he wanted her too much. He remembered his mother doing that. Shying away from his father if he ever tried to touch her. Around the waist, on the hand, any physical affection was forbidden, for her sons as well.

Was Charlotte right, though, that the only way they would have a successful marriage would be if they shared their feelings? What a foreign concept.

A knock sounded on his study door, and he called "Enter," expecting the butler.

Instead, his beautiful wife breezed into the room wearing a lovely walking dress of pale green.

"Charlotte!" He stood and greeted her with a bow.

Charlotte smiled that gorgeous, cheeky smile, moved around the desk, pushed him down into his chair and climbed onto his lap. Before Archie had time even to react, she planted a quick kiss on his lips and twined her arms around his neck.

"Good morning again, Archie."

He swallowed painfully and the lump in his throat threatened his composure. This couldn't last, could it? She looked so happy to see him, and she couldn't seem to keep her hands off him. Could he have found what Oliver had? Instead of thinking about it, he pulled Charlotte closer and kissed her thoroughly, teasing her tongue with his until she giggled.

"I was hoping to go for a picnic luncheon. Would you show me your home?" She shot him an impish smile.

Archie looked out his window for the first time that morning and noticed the sunshine.

"Of course, what time?" he asked, not sure how close they were to lunchtime and not wanting to let her go so that he could look at his pocket watch.

"Now, if you're not too busy?" Charlotte arched an eyebrow in challenge.

Archie smiled and nodded in acceptance. Of course, he had things to do, but this was his honeymoon, wasn't it?

They made their way on foot along one of the many paths around the lake, until they found a tree with sufficient shade from the sun. Ever afraid of sunspots, Charlotte had brought her parasol, but didn't wish to hold it over herself whilst she ate.

Archie happily laid out the picnic rug and arranged the food on it. The cook had put together pieces of cold chicken, sandwiches, fruit and even some cold apple cakes.

Archie waited for her to sit and then lay down opposite her. He told her about the history of his home and the number of tenants and responsibilities that came with the estate. He didn't think he had ever talked so much or been so at ease with another person before. And to have that with Charlotte was beyond his wildest dreams.

"So, tell me why you changed your mind about us marrying?" Charlotte asked once he'd stopped talking.

Archie's good mood shattered. He didn't want to have that conversation right now, nor think about that time of his life ever again. But he knew she deserved to hear the truth.

"I just couldn't lie to myself anymore."

"What do you mean?" Charlotte asked, stretching out her hand and drawing his into her own.

Archie felt the reassuring touch of her fingers and drew in a steadying breath. He had been waiting for this question for the last few days. Because of her pregnancy, he'd never had the chance to explain just why he had been so stubborn about not marrying her. Now that he had to tell her, he didn't want to. He wanted to forget the last twenty-seven years of his life and focus on the next forty.

"I thought I could live without you, but I was wrong. I was miserable, and I just couldn't bear it any longer."

"So, you did lie to me..." Charlotte's voice trailed off, but he knew exactly what she was asking.

"Yes, I lied. I told you I didn't love you, but I did. Will you forgive me?" He asked the most important question of his life and held his breath, his pulse beating hard in his ears.

Charlotte bent her head and softly kissed Archie's lips. "Of course," she whispered. Straightening up again, she added, "Although I still don't understand why you didn't marry me five years ago."

Archie laughed; he couldn't help it. He had been wondering the same thing.

"Would you have married me if I had asked you five years ago?"

Charlotte tilted her head to the side and stared at him. "Maybe. If you'd shown me the true you."

Archie thought about that. He probably wouldn't have. She'd been so young, and he had been so scared of breaking even one rule. She would have likely concluded that he was a boring individual and would not have bothered.

"Maybe it's better that we are together now, rather than then," Archie murmured, looking down at the delicate white hand in his.

"Yes, but you had to go through that horrible time alone. Thinking you had lost everyone. I could have helped you." Charlotte dropped her gaze to her lap, where she picked at her apple cake.

"Charlotte, you did help me. If you hadn't come to my study that day, I could still be in my self-made hell." Archie told her, his heart sick at the thought.

It was almost impossible to remember that this same day last week he was barely eating, trying to simply survive from one minute to the next. Now, he was sitting in the sunshine with his new wife, the only woman he had ever wanted, or loved.

Charlotte looked up and gave him one of her best smiles.

"But why were you so worried then?"

Archie sighed. Charlotte was so optimistic. She always had been.

"Because I still think that you are going to suffer because you have married me. I'm sure you heard people talking about my family and me when you were in London. How are you going to feel when people start whispering about you, or me? What if you heard that I had the same illness as my brother?"

Archie was voicing his worst fears, and his stomach was getting tighter with every word. "I could never live with you hating me."

Charlotte took a deep breath and her blue eyes darkened.

"Archie, you are my husband, and you are now my priority. You and our child. I will never listen to any idle gossip about you and not defend you. Your brother has died of a horrible disease but that has nothing, and I mean nothing, to do with you."

Archie looked at her angry expression and felt a slightly hysterical laugh bubbling up. "But what if society refuses me, us?"

"Oh, who cares about society?" She waved her hand dismissively.

"You do," he answered. She had spent her whole life in the ballrooms of the haute *ton*, wouldn't she miss it?

"I've never cared what they thought about me. I only spent so much time there because it staved off the boredom."

Archie gave her a confused look, and she sighed.

"Archie, you don't realise that as women we are educated only to the point where we can entertain a room full of people and run a home once we are married. I couldn't go to my club, I couldn't run an estate, I wasn't married, and I did not have a child. What else was I supposed to do?"

Archie thought about this and realised he had never really considered what life would be like for a lady of his class. Their choices were very limited.

"So, if we are cut off, you won't hate me?"

Charlotte laughed; the sound slightly shocking to Archie when they were discussing something so serious.

"Archie, I love you. Even if we are completely shunned, which I don't think will happen, I would be happy to stay here forever. I will have you, our baby, and a beautiful home where our friends and family can visit any time."

Archie sat up now, unable to believe his ears. Why hadn't he trusted her? Why hadn't he simply asked her what she wanted? He could have saved them both so much pain.

He went up onto his knees and moved over to kiss her.

"I LOVE YOU," he whispered against her lips. Archie kissed her so sweetly, tears slipped unheralded down her cheeks.

The familiar stirrings of desire swirled within her belly, but she was still very sore. She wasn't sure if it was the pregnancy or the amount of penetration from the night before, but she was much sorer than after their first time together.

Pulling away from their kiss, she encouraged Archie to lay with his head in her lap. Stroking his brow and silky-smooth hair, he closed his eyes, obviously at peace. They stayed that way for most of the afternoon.

After another beautiful dinner, they retired separately. Charlotte wanted another bath, and Archie needed to write a letter of business.

After her bath, Charlotte dressed in her sheerest nightgown and walked next door to Archie's rooms. Slipping into his bed, she sat up and against the many pillows and waited for him.

He arrived ten minutes later, his surprise at her presence obvious.

"I thought you might not want to share a bed tonight," he crooned, shedding his clothes, one item at a time.

Charlotte just smiled, pleased she had read her husband correctly. He would not have come to her if she had stayed in her room, and that would just not do. She was still quite sore but knew there were other ways to please her husband than with her "honey pot," as he called it. She blushed just thinking the phrase, and Archie noticed.

"What are you thinking about?" he asked her, a beautiful smile spreading over his handsome face.

"I was wondering what you usually wore to bed," Charlotte answered, which wasn't a total lie. She wanted to know what she would have to strip off him.

"I don't usually wear anything to bed. Would you like me to wear a night-shirt?" he asked respectfully and reached into a drawer.

She laughed. There was no way she was being denied the feel of his hot, smooth skin against hers.

"No, I want you to sleep as you always do."

"But..." Archie trailed off, his eyebrows drawing together in thought.

She continued to stare at him, so he nodded and slowly stripped himself of all of his clothes and stepped toward her.

Charlotte slid out of bed and stood in front of the fire in her white night-gown that cleverly hinted at the body beneath. She beckoned him with her eyes.

He quirked an eyebrow in question and took a deep breath. Charlotte was enthralled. Archie had the most magnificent body. Lean and muscular with beautiful thick legs and a flat belly. His member was already thickening and rising even as she looked at it.

"Let's get into bed," Archie suggested, taking her hand to lead her there.

Charlotte let him guide her back to bed, but only so she could watch him walk. His vitals swung, and he seemed to be getting control of his body. That just wouldn't do, either.

Archie crawled beneath the covers, pulling the blankets up to his chin. Charlotte grabbed the sheer layers of her nightdress and pulled it over her head. Archie made a choking noise and sat up. Charlotte watched her husband carefully for indications of how he felt. She was completely naked, with her back to the warm fire.

"Charlotte, I thought we should have a night off from lovemaking. You're still too sore." His voice sounded strange, as though he were choking.

"I am still sore. I wasn't going to make love to you."

She whipped the blankets back down his legs and saw his fully extended member. She chuckled happily. At least she knew he still liked her appearance.

"Charlotte, please stop torturing me." Archie groaned as his hands clenched spasmodically, forming fists at his sides.

Charlotte crawled onto the bed and kissed her husband. She slid her tongue into his mouth, and he moaned again, letting her tongue play with his, sliding together, giving each other pleasure.

Charlotte exerted pressure on Archie's chest and pushed him flat.

"Stay there. It's my turn to show you how much I love you," she commanded.

Archie smiled hesitantly and lay back.

Chapter Nineteen

Charlotte surveyed the beautiful body spread out before her and wondered if she could put her mouth straight down onto him. Looking back at his face, she thought he might not be amenable to that. Better to work up to it.

She knelt beside him and ran her hands over his little pink nipples and his broad, lightly hairy chest. Archie moaned and closed his eyes, his face showing signs of pleasure and happiness. She lay down next to him and began kissing his body. She first touched her lips to each nipple and then down the middle of his chest.

Slowly, inch by inch, she moved closer and closer to her target. She could hear Sarah's voice in her head. "When you love someone, you want to please them," so Charlotte kept kissing. Around his navel, down to the curly, rough hairs that guarded his sex.

"Charlotte, I don't think you should kiss down there." Archie's voice was strained.

She stopped and looked up. Archie had his eyes closed and was talking through clenched teeth.

What had Sarah said? *"Oliver said that most ladies don't."* So, that was the problem. Archie was still worried about doing the right thing by society.

"Why not?" she asked, wrapping her palm around him and giving his flesh a long, slow tug with her hand.

Archie groaned, and his hips flexed up.

"Because you're not meant to," Archie hissed out, still speaking through his clenched teeth.

Charlotte giggled and kissed his lips. Archie groaned and opened his eyes.

She tilted her head and set her lips to his hard flesh. He watched with wide open eyes as she kissed up and down the shaft.

"Charlotte, ladies aren't supposed to..." He trailed off as she licked the large smooth head of his member.

Charlotte laughed again and waited for him to look at her. This was a lot more pleasant than she had expected.

"Archie, I am your wife, and I want to. You do this to me, so I should do it to you."

"But..."

"Archie, have you ever put this inside another woman?" she asked sharply, gripping the base of his thick shaft as firmly as she dared.

"No, you know I haven't!"

"And do you intend to?" Charlotte asked, stroking him slowly, trying to confuse him as much as possible.

"No, of course not," he answered, closing his eyes.

"Then since I am your one and only lover, I should fulfill your every need, as you do for me."

Charlotte saw the worry still evident in her husband's eyes and did the only other thing she could think of. She twirled around so that she could still kiss him but so that he could touch her, too.

"I am still sore, so be careful, but I want you to feel how much I like doing this. My body can't lie. Neither can yours."

And with that, she spread her legs slightly, and opened her lips and sucked the pink head fully into her mouth.

Archie groaned as he stroked his fingertip over the small nub of her pleasure and she moaned low in her throat. Seeking confirmation that she was enjoying herself, he slipped his fingers slowly between her legs and found her so wet that he gasped.

Charlotte turned to look at him and smiled. "See?"

Then she began in earnest. She gripped the base of his penis in one hand and started sucking at the other end.

"Charlotte, please stop, I'm going to come if you keep doing that."

Perfect. Charlotte sucked harder and started pulling at his flesh with her hand.

She sensed the tightening of Archie's body and felt one of his hands hold her head closer. So she moved at a pace, as though she was making love to him.

He groaned like his soul was being ripped from him. His pleasure exploded into her mouth and Charlotte swallowed the salty taste of him on reflex, licking the tip and sucking him one more time.

Archie made loud gasping noises and threw an arm over his sweaty brow.

Charlotte smiled to herself and maneuvered around him. She curled into her sleeping position on the side, waiting for Archie to "spoon" her.

He moved sluggishly, but managed to pull up the quilt, covering them both. He curled his hot, strong body around hers. He sighed and kissed her hair.

"Thank you," he whispered into her ear.

"You're very welcome." Charlotte sighed, pulling his arm around to rest on their child.

She fell instantly asleep with the knowledge that she had just fully satisfied her husband.

THEY CONTINUED this way for the next three months. Talking during the day and spending their nights learning the secrets of each other's bodies.

Charlotte had taken to writing letters to friends and family most days and having frequent naps in the afternoons. This gave Archie plenty of time for estate business and his horses. He promised her he would teach her to ride, once she was no longer pregnant.

Charlotte's pregnancy was going beautifully. Almost five months along, her belly was a hard, rounded swelling, jutting out between her hips. Archie loved the changes in her body and told her so frequently that Charlotte could never feel upset or disconcerted about the vastly different curves.

The nausea was gone, and Charlotte's healthy appetite was back. For food as well as her husband. He was insatiable. Archie would make love to her morning, noon and night if she allowed him, and occasionally she did.

The first test of their marriage came in the form of an invitation.

Archie knocked on the door of what was now Charlotte's morning sitting room. She sat at her embroidery. He entered to find her singing softly to their baby.

She raised her head. "Yes, my love?" Charlotte frowned slightly at his expression. "Are you all right?" she asked, moving to stand.

"No, don't get up." He stopped her, sitting in the chair opposite hers.

He unfolded the invitation in his hand and offered it to her.

"We've been invited to the christening of Oliver and Sarah's son," Archie explained unnecessarily, as Charlotte read the invitation herself.

"Oh, that's wonderful. Two weeks. Well, that gives us plenty of time to pack and travel to London. I need to order a few new dresses, too," she explained, rubbing her belly with a satisfied smile.

Archie stopped short. He wasn't sure if he wanted to go and he didn't know how to explain that to his wife. He had worked out that he could drop to half mourning the same weekend as the christening, but it would be the first public event he would attend since his brother's death.

"You want to go?" Archie croaked, his nerves getting the best of him.

He had lost the easy ability to disguise how he was feeling around his wife. Charlotte had worn down all resistance with her constant questions and attention. He liked to think he had helped her, too. She glowed with love, and he enjoyed the idea that he put that light there.

"Of course. Don't you?" Charlotte's eyes were wide with surprise.

"I'd like to go, but it will be the first event since my brother's death." Archie hoped she wouldn't need a better explanation than that.

Charlotte studied his face for a moment, before speaking.

"Archie, we don't have to go, not if you don't want to."

He let out a breath he didn't know he had been holding.

"But it would be very rude of us to decline without a proper reason. After all, the Duke and Duchess of Lincoln have specially invited us," Charlotte reminded him with a smile.

Archie clenched his teeth. He knew he was being herded the way Charlotte wanted to go, but didn't know how to fight her. Yes, it would be rude to decline an invitation from not only his best friend, but also one of the most powerful families in London.

"Charlotte, what if you are treated badly because of your marriage to me?" Archie voiced his most profound fear.

Charlotte laughed. "Archie, I love you. If anyone wants to cut me from society because I married you, then I am happy never to speak to them again. Our friends want to see us, and that is what's important."

Archie considered her words and watched her eyes and face for evidence that she was lying. He saw none and exhaled slowly. If Charlotte was willing to brave the *ton*'s censure, then who was he to be scared? He was the one who had been preparing for it for the past ten years. What was he really worried about? He swallowed audibly and asked the one question that terrified him.

"And no matter what, you won't stop loving me?"

He dropped his eyes to the floor, unable to hold her gaze. Despite the desperate need to see her face when she answered, his fear of seeing something he didn't like was greater.

Standing up, Charlotte moved over to Archie and forced her way onto his lap. She put one hand on Archie's chin to pull his eyes up to hers, and she used the other hand to guide his to her burgeoning belly.

"Archie, I have said this before, and I will say it every day if you need to hear it. I love you. Nothing will make me turn away from you, ever."

Pushing his hand harder into her bump, she continued. "You and this baby are my whole world, and I will happily give you as many children as you want. So that we can have a loving family like neither of us had."

Archie blinked several times, forcing hot tears away. Was it possible?

"Archie, you have made me happier than I ever imagined possible. If you keep it up, I promise I will stand by you through anything."

He felt himself beginning to hope. Just like the sun coming through the cracks in the clouds on a winter's day, her words filtered through the fog of his uncertainty. He smiled softly and felt a tear slip down his cheek.

Their baby chose that moment to give its first big kick, right under Archie's hand.

"Oh, did you feel that?" Charlotte grabbed his hand and pushed down even harder.

Archie felt the armour around his heart shatter, as his heart swelled with love for this woman. For Charlotte, who had dragged him, kicking and screaming, into the sunshine.

"I love you," he whispered pulling her face to his for a kiss that had his body aching for her.

"Come to bed," Charlotte whispered against Archie's lips, standing up and pulling him with her.

Archie fought the urge to throw his wife over his shoulder and run up the stairs. Only her belly stopped him.

"Lead the way, my lady." He bowed with a cheeky smile.

They travelled to London the following week.

LONDON HAD NEVER LOOKED BRIGHTER to Charlotte. She was married, with child, and loved beyond comparison. What else could make her life better? Well, perhaps, not being shunned by people who had known her, her whole life. That would be a good start. She had never been so disgusted with the *ton*'s behaviour before.

They had arrived in London a few days before, and Charlotte had instantly set out to order new gowns to accommodate her expanding figure. She had been asked to come back at a later time when the shop was closed, so that people wouldn't know that she frequented that modiste. Charlotte had stormed out and instead found a small but beautiful shop with an English modiste.

"I am the new Countess of Tother," she announced to the modiste. "Would you like my business?"

The young lady had blinked and curtseyed.

"Indeed, I would like that, your ladyship. Can I get you a cup of tea?"

Charlotte had a little cry, to be perfectly honest, and then proceeded to order more gowns than she could wear in a season. She had money, and Archie thought she was beautiful. She would have the best of everything.

Driving home in her carriage, she started to realise that Archie had been right to worry about society's reaction to them. She had known, of course, what might happen, but to be affronted by a shop lady was just too much.

She pasted a bright smile on her face and swept into her new townhouse.

"Good day, my lady," their ancient butler said, and bowed deeply.

Charlotte blushed brightly. She still hadn't become accustomed to seeing the man who knew exactly when and where she had first made love to Archie. The poor man looked just as uncomfortable every time he saw her, but Charlotte wouldn't have changed him for the world. He ran a tight ship, and he had saved her several times from embarrassing or insulting visitors.

"Is his lordship in the study?" Charlotte asked, pulling off her cloak and gloves. She handed them to a waiting footman.

"Yes. Mister Rupert is with him."

The old butler's mouth turned down slightly, and Charlotte suppressed a smile. The butler was a stickler for tradition and disapproved of Rupert's flagrant disrespect for drinking hours and his disrespect toward married women.

Rupert had visited on their first day in London and had given Charlotte a loud, smacking kiss on the mouth in congratulations. The poor butler had almost expired on the spot. Truth be told, Archie hadn't been too impressed either. But Charlotte knew Rupert's weakness now, and she would stop the rake in his tracks.

"Thank you, Hill," she said, gliding up to the door of the study.

She heard two male voices within, and a laugh she recognised as her husband's. It was wonderful to hear him so happy.

She knocked once and pushed open the heavy door.

Both gentlemen jumped to their feet on her entry. Rupert gave her a sly smile and looked at Archie.

"Countess," Rupert greeted her, stepping forward to touch her, in goodness knows what way.

Instead of moving toward him, Charlotte flattened her palms on her belly and pulled the dress taut around the prominent bump.

"Hello Rupert," she greeted him with a serene, Madonna-like smile.

Rupert stopped in his tracks, his eyes falling to her belly. He flushed noticeably and straightened to his full, imposing height.

"You are looking very well, my dear," Archie said, as he walked forward and greeted her with a bow and a kiss to her outstretched fingers. For good measure, he ran his hand possessively over his growing child.

She heard Rupert's throat gurgle, though she was unsure whether it was with amusement, or embarrassment.

"I've been shopping," Charlotte announced, with the air of someone very important.

"Oh, no," Archie groaned dramatically. "Please tell me there is enough money left to pay the servants."

Charlotte just laughed and sat down.

Archie looked at Rupert with alarm, but Rupert only laughed.

"You're lucky you don't have any sisters," he said.

Rupert had three sisters and more than ten nieces. He was surrounded by women.

"I found a new dressmaker who is making everything I need for the Season. She also recommended a baby shop I'm going to visit tomorrow."

"That sounds great, love," Archie said absently, moving back to his chair. "New dressmaker? I thought you only wanted to go to that French modiste on Bond Street. You've been waiting for three days to see her."

Charlotte flushed but refused to look away from her husband's keen stare.

"That shopkeeper decided I wasn't important enough to serve on priority, so I found one who wants my business."

Archie gave her a startled look, and even Rupert looked uncomfortable as he, too, took his chair.

"Do you mean to tell me you were denied service because of your new status?"

"Not at all. She was still happy to make my clothes, but she didn't want me seen in her presence. So, I refused to go back, and found someone more than happy to have me patronise her shop." Charlotte told them both the honest truth.

"You were denied access because of me," Archie choked out.

Rupert stood up and bowed.

"I think I'll be going, Archie. I'll see you at the christening on Sunday." Rupert gave Charlotte an apologetic smile. She didn't blame him for wanting to leave such a conversation.

"Yes, indeed," Archie recovered enough to say, the look in his eyes showing his mind was far away.

Rupert headed for the door, but as he opened it, he turned back to say something. "We still love you both," he said. With that rather shocking statement, he fled.

Charlotte smiled fondly as the rogue ran for cover.

"He has a heart of gold somewhere under all that swagger. I'm sure of it," Charlotte declared, laughing despite herself.

Archie dropped to his knees in front of her and kissed her tenderly for a moment, before pulling away once again. He sat in the chair closest to her.

"Tell me what happened today. Did they upset you?" Archie asked, holding her hands in a time-old gesture of support.

"I am the daughter of a duchess and a future marchioness, Archibald. No one upsets me," she declared as haughtily as possible.

Her husband knew her too well to believe it. "They did," he said, sitting down in his chair and pulling her down onto his lap.

"Archie, please don't be upset. It's true, I was a little shocked, but it doesn't matter."

"It does!"

Charlotte gave up and just kissed him. Kissed him until they were both panting and desperate.

He made love to her right there, in the study, where it had begun, all those months ago.

Chapter Twenty

After Charlotte's traumatic experience of buying a new gown, Archie decided to find out just how bad the situation was.

He went to his club the next day, dressed in full mourning, but very fashionable clothes. He was lucky enough to find John instantly and sat down with him. The club was quiet, owing to this time being the end of the Season and Archie was grateful. His jumping belly and sweating palms were great indications that he was suddenly feeling not so courageous.

"Archie." John greeted him with an enthusiastic handshake and cleared his throat.

"I saw Charlotte this morning. She is looking wonderful."

Archie blinked. He hadn't realised Charlotte had visited her parents alone. He had been too busy with his bank manager this morning to even ask her about her plans.

"She is," Archie agreed quietly, his eyes darting to a man in the corner of the room who was giving them black looks.

"I'm not sure if I should be sitting with you, John," Archie apologised, beginning to rise.

John grabbed him by the sleeve and unceremoniously hauled him back down.

"Archie, you're not only my best friend, but my brother-in-law as well. If you should be sitting anywhere, it is here." John called for port, and a footman scurried over with two glasses.

Archie picked his up and drank it in one gulp, the burn making him gasp and hiss.

John chuckled and called for more.

"Don't tell me, married life isn't as good as Oliver makes it out to be," John joked, watching Archie as he gulped down more port.

Archie almost choked and put his glass back down with a hurry.

"No, Charlotte's wonderful," Archie answered quietly, twirling his glass between his palms. He did not look up, until the liquid warmth began to help his cold belly.

John cleared his throat meaningfully, and Archie dragged his eyes up to see an old friend of his father's standing in front of them.

"You shouldn't be here, Turner," the man said to Archie, his head held high, a walking stick gripped in one hand.

"I have every right to be here, sir," Archie replied respectfully. He stood and bowed to the older man. He wasn't being shown any manners, but he hadn't forgotten his.

"Your brother was a disgrace." The old man glared at him, obviously eager to get to the crux of the matter.

Archie nodded his head once in agreement. He couldn't help feeling the hypocrisy of the situation. The men in this room were the very worst whore-mongering rogues and yet his brother was a disgrace?

"I'm going to ask the club to bar your admittance." The older man snarled now, his lip quivering in his anger.

Several of the other older men exchanged looks amongst themselves. Some were resolute, ready to back him up, others seemed embarrassed and worried.

"You must do what you must do," Archie declared, comfortable in his ostracism.

John stood up next to him.

"Then you can ask for my membership to be rescinded too. Because the day the future Marquess of Hunting is barred from this club, is the day I have no wish to be a part of this club."

The reminder of who Archie would be in the future, seemed to deflate some of the older man's anger. John's presence took care of the rest.

John threw some money down onto the table and gave Archie a look that said that it was time to leave.

They gathered their coats and left without speaking.

They decided to walk back to their townhouses rather than taking a carriage. Along the way, Archie gathered his courage and spoke to his friend. "Thank you, John, but you don't need to lose your position for me."

John harrumphed and kept walking. He was mumbling under his breath, and Archie couldn't help the slightly hysterical laugh that escaped his throat.

"What's so funny?" John asked, scowling at him as they made their way along the street.

"Nothing, nothing at all. It's just that, after ten years of waiting for the worst to happen, it has. And you have stood by me."

John flushed, his handsome face becoming pink in a way Archie had never seen it.

"Archie, you're not your brother. You have proven that a hundred times over the last ten years."

"But the *ton* doesn't recognise that," Archie pointed out.

"Blast the *ton*," John muttered, walking even faster and kicking at the cobblestones with his polished black boots.

Archie walked along the road next to his brother-in-law and wondered why he wasn't angrier. He should be, after all. He'd lost everything he once valued. The respect of his peers and his place in society.

But the warmth of the sunshine on his face, and John beside him, gave him a greater sense of self-worth than he'd ever had. Something he must ponder for a while.

ARCHIE GOT HOME to the message that his wife was feeling ill. He rushed straight to their room to find her not there. On enquiry, he found the countess asleep in her bed. *Her* bed! They hadn't slept apart in almost four months and tonight she had decided they would?

Archie stood at the door that linked their rooms and paused with his hand on the knob. How could he go to her when he had been asked not to do so? Their marriage was strange, in that she had always come to his bed, not he to hers. He knew that all husbands across the English aristocracy had separate bedrooms and only visited their wives when required. It had never been that way for them, and it felt horrible now.

Archie moved back to his lonely bed and climbed, naked, into it. He had slept in this bed alone for more than ten years, and yet tonight it felt as cold and as empty as a Scottish loch. Archie pulled the blankets around him tighter and shivered.

What could he do? Perhaps Charlotte truly wasn't well? And if so, why didn't she tell him so herself, or at least allow him to hold her.

It was true, they had never spent a night in each other's arms without making love, or some variation of intimacy. But that didn't mean he couldn't control himself. Perhaps that was it? Perhaps she was sore, or tired, and was scared to rebuff him in bed? If that were so, he would strive to be a more considerate husband. Perhaps he had worn her out the previous night? He cringed at the memory. Or this morning when he had made love to her again?

He had known that the honeymoon would not last; he had just foolishly believed that she had been as happy as he.

The next morning, Archie arose early and set out for a ride. He rarely rode in London, but he needed to get out into the fresh air today. He rode around the parks and over as many hills as he could find. When the horse was tired, Archie headed home and went straight to his study. He attacked all the estate business he had put off and tried very hard not to think about what he would say to his wife later that day.

THAT EVENING, dinner was a stilted affair. Neither of them seemed to know what to say. Charlotte was dumbfounded. The only conversation went along distant, polite lines.

"Are you feeling better today, Charlotte?"

"I am, thank you, Archie," she said and then silence fell again.

Charlotte retired to her bed but sat up waiting for her husband. She was testing him again. She had never slept in her new bed before yesterday and yet Archie didn't seem annoyed by the sudden change.

Snuffing out her candle finally, she burrowed down into her bed with a small sob. Why wouldn't he come to her? She buried her head into her pillow and started crying.

Minutes later, Archie thrust open the door and walked straight into her room. He was carrying a candle and wearing a nightshirt. Charlotte looked up at his entrance and blinked. Archie put the candle down on his side of the bed and put his hand on the covers. He didn't make any move to slide into the bed, just quirked an eyebrow.

Relief and love overflowed within her. "Oh, Archie," she sobbed, holding out her arms for him.

Archie pulled back the covers and climbed in next to her. He sat up against the pillows and pulled Charlotte into his strong arms. She burst into a fresh round of tears and sobbed on his chest. Archie held her whilst she cried and cried, crooning and stroking her hair.

"I'm sorry I didn't come sooner."

"I just want you to love me, nothing else matters." Charlotte burst out into hysterical sobs. All she wanted was her husband's love. Why had she felt the need to test him?

Archie lay back against the pillows and pulled Charlotte to him. She was no longer sobbing, but she still clung to him in desperation.

"I love you, Charlotte. I'm sorry I haven't been here for you."

She shook her head against him, wiping at her dripping nose and eyes. "No, no, please don't be sorry. That's what I didn't want."

Archie sighed and held her tighter. "Just sleep, my love."

Charlotte fell asleep almost instantly, the exhaustion of the previous day's emotional upheaval too much for her. Archie loved her, and that was all that mattered.

THE FOLLOWING Sunday was David's christening. Archie wore half-mourning, and Charlotte chose a beautiful pale blue dress from her new dressmaker. Archie was relieved that their marriage appeared to be back to normal. They had made love all morning and were both in high spirits.

"I cannot believe you are showing your face here."

Charlotte and Archie both turned to find a richly dressed older lady glaring at them.

"We were invited," Archie calmly replied. He didn't even know the woman in front of him. How could he have offended her?

"Then you should have refused. You shouldn't be allowed to enter society after what your brother did."

Archie felt his stomach drop but took strength in the solid warmth of his wife next to him.

"My brother has paid for his crimes, my lady, unlike most men of the *ton*. Don't you agree that death was payment enough?"

"Yes, I do actually, but what about you?" the old woman snapped again.

"Me?" Archie let his eyebrows rise comically high on his forehead.

"Yes, how dare you marry Lady Charlotte? She could have married anyone she wanted, and you chose to drag her into a family that is diseased. You could give it to her, or her child."

The lady eyed Charlotte's waistline critically and smiled smugly.

"And that is not a three-month belly. So, either you married her when she was with child by someone else, or you are as bad as your brother." The old woman, who in her day would have been very handsome, was smiling nastily now.

Archie felt anger, hurt, and embarrassment in equal quantities, and was finding it hard to work out which emotion was strongest. Heat flooded his face and chest making it hard to breathe.

But before he could open his mouth to answer the old battleaxe, he felt Charlotte's hand on his arm, squeezing tightly.

"I married Archie because I love him," she declared hotly, her sincerity ringing out clearly. "His poor brother was unlucky but was not unusual in his habits, as I'm sure you know. Also, I wouldn't be casting stones regarding the size of my belly. Your daughter had a six-month babe, if my memory serves, and I can guarantee you, at least I know who the father of my child is."

Archie choked on a laugh, and he had the unseemly urge to clap. His wife was incredible. Absolutely wonderful.

The old battleaxe began choking on her bitterness, her face turning an ugly shade of purple as she screwed up her face.

Charlotte pulled herself up to her full height and looked down at the old dragon.

"If you will excuse us, we need to find a good place to sit so that we can watch the christening of our friend's child."

Archie would be told many years later that no one there that day remembered anything else that was said. Except for the fact that Lady Charlotte was indeed in love with her husband and would happily fight off anyone who dared speak ill of him. No one else tried.

Archie looked up proudly from his seat as his dearest friend spoke out from the front of the church.

"Thank you for attending the christening of our son, David. The duchess' family have a tradition that they only inform the chosen godparents of their child on the day of the christening."

There was a general murmur of agreement from Sarah's extended family and silence from the rest of the *ton*. It was most unusual.

"We decided to stick with tradition and have not told our friends that we have chosen them."

Oliver smiled hugely, and the collective group held their breaths. It would be a great honour to be named godparent to the heir to the Duke of Lincoln. The *ton* knew Oliver and Sarah had a highly unorthodox marriage, and Archie understood that no one would be entirely surprised they had chosen to adhere to some alternative tradition.

"We would like to invite the godparents to the front of the church. The Earl and Countess of Tother."

Oliver and Sarah both beamed and looked expectantly at their chosen champions for their son.

Archie's heart leapt, and his wife's hand tightened in his. How could they do this? They had just been shunned by the better half of the *ton* and now were given the greatest honour that could be bestowed on two people.

Archie looked down at his beautiful, loyal and loving wife. He smiled. If Charlotte believed in him, and Oliver and Sarah believed in them as a couple, who was he to try to refute that? He stood up, gently pulling his wife up next to him, and together they walked up the aisle.

They moved to the front of the church and thanked the Duke and Duchess of Lincoln, their beautiful friends, Oliver and Sarah. Archie calmly took their firstborn child and heir in his arms and proceeded to renounce Satan and promise to raise David as a loyal Christian.

Archie spent the entire service outside his body looking down. How could he have ever thought he could live a life without his friends and family by his side? How could he have ever imagined that Charlotte couldn't overcome anything that life could throw at her?

He would one day be the Marquess of Hunting. He was wealthy, handsome and healthy. He had a wife who was surpassed by none, and she loved him as much as he loved her. Life couldn't be any sweeter.

Epilogue

Five years later

"Archie, if you don't get this book off my table..." Charlotte began yelling at him.

She was cranky as she always was when she was almost nine months heavy with child. Her third child in five years, to be precise.

"I'm sorry, Charlotte. I shouldn't have left it there," Archie said quickly, picking up his book on stud farms and tucking it under his arm.

He had only put it down for a moment so that he could pick up William, their four-year-old son, and then he had become distracted.

They already had two sons, William, who was four, and George, who was two. They were both wonderful children, boisterous and full of life. William looked just like him, with intense brown eyes and a beautiful smile. He was quieter than his brother and liked to have his parents read to him.

George was more like his mother in both looks and personality. He had a temper that could bring the house down, and blue eyes that could melt your heart.

Archie knew that Charlotte was hoping for a girl this time, and he couldn't help hoping for the same. He wanted a little girl with Charlotte's face and maybe a little of his personality. Another George in temperament and they were in trouble. Each child already had a nursemaid, but if they got a baby girl with Charlotte's personality, they would be hiring another one.

Charlotte was a wonderful mother, attentive and kind. She loved spending time with the boys and could usually be found reading them stories in the nursery or running around with them outside. However, as she was due to give birth to their third child any day, she was as large as a house, and as cranky as Archie had ever seen her.

"Perhaps I could coax you into having a lie-down?" Archie asked with a suggestive smile. They hadn't made love in weeks, and he knew it would be months until he could touch her again.

Charlotte gave him a startled expression that soon changed into something more serene.

"Yes," she declared, putting out her hand so that he could help her to her feet.

Archie pulled up his wife as gently as he could and then saw a very unusual look on Charlotte's face.

"What's wrong, my love?"

"I need the midwife, Archie," she explained, putting her hand to her belly as the first cramp hit.

"Oh, oh!" Archie exclaimed, towing his wife gently up the stairs before sending for the midwife who was stationed in the village.

Six hours later, Archie was holding his new baby daughter, Lady Sarah Claire Turner. She had brilliant blue eyes and a mop of black curls. Archie's heart had melted a little when he had met his sons, but the moment he met his daughter, he knew he could never love anyone more.

"She's perfect, Charlotte," he whispered, two tears slipping down his cheeks.

Charlotte sighed and lay back against her pillows.

"As perfect as you are, my love," she whispered before she drifted off to sleep for a hard-earned rest.

THE END

Download book 3 now:
https://books2read.com/u/31erow

Or read on for a sneak peek into the next story in 'The Heir and the Spare' series.

Lizzie's Recalcitrant Earl

Chapter One

London 1813

Rupert Willoughby was strikingly handsome. Or so he'd been told, since before he'd left the cradle. The combination of truly blue eyes and black hair had enticed many a beauty into his bed.

Thanks to his brother's wealth and generosity, he had an excellent allowance. Rupert's best friend, the former Lord Archibald Turner, now the Earl of Tother, an original member of their group, "the spares," was a dab hand at the Stock Exchange. Archie often advised Rupert about how to invest his money and thus, he was set for the future. Rupert would never have to seek employment as so many second sons had to do.

He secretly wanted a wife such as his friends Archie, Earl of Tother, and Oliver, Duke of Lincoln, had found. Sarah, Duchess of Lincoln, and Charlotte, Countess of Tother, were both ladies who could hold an intelligent conversation and also manage a household. Women who were beautiful, but much more than merely decorative. Rupert wasn't sure if he would ever find such a woman for himself and certainly not one who could hold his interest in the bedchamber. It would probably be better to find a 'suitable" wife and continue to live as he already did. As long as he produced the required heir, his responsibilities would be met.

At the Duke and Duchess of Lincoln's annual ball, Rupert eyed the beauty talking to the Countess of Tother. The former Lady Charlotte Dunford looked very well. Beautiful, in fact. She was still quite blissfully happy with her marriage to his friend, Archie, Earl of Tother, and if Rupert wasn't mistaken, could very well be *enceinte* again. Unlike many of the women of the *ton* who all but hid throughout their pregnancies, Charlotte glowed with good health and happily stood in the centre of a crowded ball-room. She had no qualms showing everyone how happy she was to be bearing another child for her husband. Rupert shook his head against the unfamiliar notion. It was confounding.

Next to her, however, was a young lady whom Rupert had never seen before. She had hair as blonde as Sarah's. She had tan skin in comparison to Charlotte's paleness, but it suited her hair. He couldn't see her eyes very well from where he was standing, but they appeared to him quite dark. She was striking. She had high cheekbones, classic features, and an amazing smile that affected him even from where he was standing, right across the room. Rarely had Rupert seen a more beautiful woman.

He noted that she was short in stature and that she had high, firm breasts, swelling above her low neckline. The blue of her dress and her wedding ring proclaimed her married. Or widowed, perhaps. Either way, she was the perfect rendezvous he needed. He was a little bored with his latest mistress.

Rupert adjusted his coat with a quick tug and straightened to his full height. Feeling confident, he walked over to the two ladies.

"May I beg you for an introduction to your friend, my dear Charlotte?"

Charlotte smiled tightly, knowing his habits well. She turned to include him in their circle, which surprised him a little, but his friend's sister did have perfect manners.

"Of course, Rupert. Mrs. Elizabeth Symmons, may I introduce a friend of ours, the Honourable Rupert Willoughby, the younger brother of the Earl of Sweeting."

Rupert heard the warning in the introduction and smirked inwardly. Charlotte was fiercely protective of those she loved. It was one of the things he liked most about her.

The beautiful blonde curtseyed prettily and gave him a sunny, open smile. Rupert bowed in return, surprised by the artlessness of her expression.

"May I have the pleasure of the next dance, my lady?" he asked, giving her his most charming smile.

Elizabeth smiled back, glancing quickly at Charlotte for permission to leave her alone, which Rupert respected. When Charlotte nodded and smiled back in return, the beautiful woman turned to him.

"Of course. Thank you, sir," she replied confidently, placing her small hand in his.

She was petite, yet Rupert felt the firmness of her grip and observed the way she held herself. This would not be a woman over whom one could easily walk, he told himself.

"You are looking charming this evening, Mrs. Symmons," Rupert told her, as they swept onto the dance floor.

Elizabeth laughed, her bright eyes sparkling with gaiety.

"Why, thank you, sir. And indeed, you are looking very handsome."

Rupert grinned, surprised by her words. He didn't believe he had ever had a compliment returned before. Most women only fluttered their fans and gave him the eyes. The eyes told him how flattered they were that he had given them his attention. The eyes also indicated to him just how quickly they would fall into his bed. Mrs. Elizabeth Symmons wasn't giving him the eyes, nor was she flirting with him. How strange.-She was difficult to read.

"How are you enjoying the evening?" Rupert asked politely, maneuvering her expertly around the many couples on the dance floor. He didn't dance often, but he considered it part of his seduction routine and therefore made sure he was rather good at it.

"Oh, I am enjoying it very much. I have recently come out of mourning and have never felt so decadent for wearing a colour before," Elizabeth explained, looking down for a moment at her beautiful blue evening gown.

Rupert smiled inwardly. A widow, was she? That was perfect. Affairs were much less stressful when there wasn't a spouse to take into consideration all the time. Would Elizabeth Symmons like just a night or two in his arms? Or would she perhaps want something more permanent? A longer time frame would work out quite nicely, Rupert thought, his mind jumping ahead with plans for her seduction.

"You must be lonely," Rupert murmured, giving her a look that was meant to be both respectful, yet meaningful to those who knew how to interpret it.

He swept his eyes subtly down to her neckline, where there was a swelling of flesh. He shifted his stance slightly, as his cock thickened in his breeches. Rupert smiled. He was surprised, but also delighted. He hadn't experienced such a strong attraction to a woman in a very long time. His body was alive, all but screaming out to lay her down on the nearest flat surface and have his wicked way with her.

His body and mind declared war. It was his primitive self, versus the cultured *ton* gentleman. If he were truly honest with himself, he had been bored for some time. Nothing was ever new or exciting anymore, but he had a feeling that this woman would be different.

"Indeed I am, my lord."

~

Read on here:
https://books2read.com/u/31erow

www.ingramcontent.com/pod-product-compliance
Lightning Source LLC
Chambersburg PA
CBHW062309200726

48292CB00004BA/1436